the YEAR of the BOMB

TO DAN, PHIL, ROBBIE, AND KEN,
AND ALWAYS TO YVONNE AND MAGGIE

Also by Ronald Kidd
Monkey Town
On Beale Street

SIMON & SCHUSTER BOOKS FOR YOUNG READERS
An imprint of Simon & Schuster Children's Publishing Division
1230 Avenue of the Americas, New York, New York 10020
This book is a work of fiction. Any references to historical events, real people, or real locales are used fictitiously. Other names, characters, places, and incidents are products of the author's imagination, and any resemblance to actual events or locales or persons, living or dead, is entirely coincidental.
SIMON & SCHUSTER BOOKS FOR YOUNG READERS is a trademark of Simon & Schuster, Inc.
Book design by Lucy Ruth Cummins
The text for this book is set in Garamond.
Manufactured in the United States of America
10 9 8 7 6 5 4 3 2 1
Library of Congress Cataloging-in-Publication Data
Kidd, Ronald.
The year of the bomb / Ronald Kidd.—1st ed.
p. cm.
Summary: In 1955 California, as *Invasion of the Body Snatchers* is
filmed in their hometown, thirteen-year-old Paul discovers a real enemy
when he and three friends go against a young government agent determined
to find communists at a nearby university or on the movie set.
ISBN: 978-1-4169-5892-5 (hardcover)
[1. Fear—Fiction. 2. Motion pictures—Production and
direction—Fiction. 3. Conduct of life—Fiction. 4. Blacklisting of
entertainers—Fiction. 5. Cold War—Fiction. 6. Family
problems—Fiction. 7. Sierra Madre (Calif.)—History—20th
century—Fiction. 8. United States—History—1953–1961—Fiction.]
I. Title.
PZ7.K5315Yec 2009
[Fic]—dc22
2008023646

the
YEAR
of the
BOMB

RONALD KIDD

SIMON & SCHUSTER BOOKS FOR YOUNG READERS
NEW YORK LONDON TORONTO SYDNEY

CONTENTS

PART ONE
THEY'RE HERE!

1 · MONSTERS ON THE LOOSE

THERE WERE MARTIANS IN THE BACKYARD.

Late one night, a flash of light woke David up. He looked out the back window and saw something floating above the fence. It looked like a flying saucer. He ran to tell his dad. His dad put on a bathrobe and went outside to check. He didn't come back.

David's mom called the police, and they searched the backyard. There was no sign of a flying saucer. But near the fence, in a sandy pit, the police found his dad's slipper. When they reached to pick it up, they were sucked down into the sand.

Later that day his dad came back. So did the police. But there was something wrong. They were acting strange. They were stiff and creepy.

Then David noticed something. On the back of their necks was a scar. Tiny electronic receivers had been surgically implanted in their spinal cords. They were being controlled by the Martians.

"Hey, Paul, you want some popcorn?"

"Huh?"

"Junior Mints? Jujubes?"

I looked up. A giant head bobbed in the darkness, like one of those balloons at the Macy's Parade. It had a grin and a crewcut. It was Crank.

"I'm watching the movie," I said.

"Can I have some?" asked a shaky voice next to me. It was Arnie, huddled in his seat with his knees up around his chin.

"No way," said Crank. "Last time, you barfed all over the floor."

"I was scared," said Arnie.

"You're always scared," said Crank.

Two seats down, Oz whispered, "Here comes the good part."

A Martian crawled out of the darkness. It had gigantic feet and a head the size of a pinball. That's because Oz had made us sit in the front row.

"Watch this," said Oz.

The Martian grabbed David, threw him over its shoulder, and disappeared into the earth.

Arnie screamed.

Crank said, "Shut up!" He slugged Arnie on the arm.

"Ow!" wailed Arnie.

"You are such a wienie," said Crank.

Arnie cowered. Crank glared. Oz grinned.

Me? I just sat there, pretending everything was fine.

But it wasn't. Flying saucers were landing. Cities were being destroyed. Monsters were on the loose. There were giant reptiles, ten-foot spiders, and dinosaurs that had escaped the bonds of time. They climbed skyscrapers. They uprooted trees. They picked up taxicabs and threw them against buildings. People ran away, shrieking. I ran with them. I'd been running for as long as I could remember.

My friends and I go to horror movies. We've seen them all: *The Thing, It Came from Outer Space, The Day the Earth Stood Still.* They scare the pee out of us. That's why we like them.

This week it was *Invaders from Mars.* We watched while the Martians carried off David, along with Patricia Blake, the beautiful doctor who had befriended him. They met the head Martian, a hideous creature who lived in a glass ball. Meanwhile, the army brought in tanks and tried to rescue them. But in the end it was David who saved the day. He grabbed a ray gun and blasted them to freedom.

When the lights came up, I checked the area for Martians. It looked safe, but you could never tell. They might be right next to you. Someone you knew could smile, then peel back his face to reveal a gaping mouth and skin that oozed and bubbled.

We stumbled outside. Arnie looked up at the bright sun. "My eyes!" he said. "I've been blinded!"

Crank swung at him again, but this time Arnie scrambled behind Oz.

"Swear to God, man," said Crank.

Oz said, "Leave him alone."

Crank stuck out his chin. "Make me."

I slid between them. They calmed down, for the moment, anyway.

My friends and I might argue about horror movies, but we would never miss them. Every week we went to see one, usually at a theater in Sierra Madre, the little town outside Los Angeles where we lived. Sometimes, though, we went to Hollywood. We would hop into our Cadillac convertible and drive there with the top down.

In our dreams.

We're thirteen years old, okay? The only convertible I own is a Schwinn. When we go to Hollywood, we either ask our parents to drive us or we take the bus.

Oz looked at his watch. "Our bus doesn't leave until four o'clock. You want to do something?"

"I'm hungry," said Crank.

I said, "What about the popcorn, Junior Mints, and Jujubes?"

He shrugged. "That was just a snack."

His name was Eugene Crookshank, but if you called him Eugene he would crush you with his bare hands. He could do it too. He was huge—not just tall, but big all over. When he walked, his shoulders swayed from side to side. Sometimes you could almost feel the ground shake. He wasn't like a monster, though. He was all right, once you got to know him. Just don't call him Eugene.

Oz said, "How about some ice cream?"

We had a lot of favorite ice-cream shops, but the best was C. C. Brown's on Hollywood Boulevard, where the hot fudge sundae had been invented. It was an old-fashioned place, with overhead fans, pink leather booths, and a floor covered with little black and white tiles.

Going inside, we settled into a booth. Crank and Arnie sat on one side, with Oz and me on the other.

"Next year is the fiftieth anniversary of C. C. Brown's," said Oz. "It was opened in 1906 by Clarence Clifton Brown."

Oz was always saying things like that. He was a walking encyclopedia. He also sounded like an encyclopedia, if that's possible. He was the shortest kid in our class, but he had the deep voice of a radio announcer. His real name was Oscar Feldman. Somewhere along the line people started calling him Oz.

The waitress came by. She looked like my uncle Ernie in a chiffon dress. When she started to hand out menus, Oz held up his hand.

"Please, don't insult us," he said. "Gentlemen?"

"Hot fudge sundae."

"Hot fudge sundae."

"Hot fudge sundae."

"And for myself," said Oz, "I think I'll have a hot fudge sundae."

She eyed us. "Wise guys, huh?"

"You have no idea," said Oz.

She gathered up the menus and left.

Arnie said, "That was scary."

"Yeah," I said, "I've never seen a waitress with a mustache."

"I meant the movie," said Arnie.

Crank stared at him. "Are you kidding? Those aliens were phony. You could see the zippers on their costumes."

"I thought it was pretty good for a low-budget film," said Oz. "The director was William Cameron Menzies. He worked on *Gone With the Wind*."

"How do you know that?" I asked. "Where do you get this stuff?"

Crank said, "He gets it from the Martians. They implanted a tiny receiver in his brain and transmit useless information. He just repeats what they say." Crank leaned forward. "Ever notice that he wears his hair longer in back? That's to cover up the surgical scar. Come on, Oz, show us the back of your neck."

"I'd rather not," said Oz.

"See that?" said Crank. "He's controlled by the aliens. When they're finished with him, they'll push a button. Ka-boom!"

"Ka-boom?" said Arnie.

"His head will explode. Blood everywhere." Crank pointed to a red stain on the table. "You thought that was ketchup? Think again."

Arnie shivered. He was Arnold Green, and ketchup

was just one of many things that scared him. According to neighborhood legend, in the fifth grade he had been so frightened about going to school that his mother used to lock him out of the house. Arnie was incredibly thin, so that when he pulled his belt tight, his pants bunched up around his waist. Some of the guys at school liked to sneak up behind him and drop pennies down the gaps. Arnie didn't mind, though. He said he could use the money.

A few minutes later, the waitress came back with a tray of sundaes and set them in front of us.

"You want anything else?" she said.

"Yeah," said Arnie. He picked up the ketchup bottle and handed it to her. "Can you take this, please?"

After we finished our sundaes, there was still an hour to kill, so we wandered down Hollywood Boulevard. We had been attacked by monsters in every movie theater there—the Egyptian, the Pantages, El Capitan, Grauman's Chinese. But Hollywood Boulevard had more than just theaters. There was Pickwick Bookshop, a three-level store with stacks as far as you could see. There was Larry Edmunds, a shop where Oz looked for movie books and posters. There was Musso & Frank's Grill, where we sneaked in sometimes looking for movie stars. Arnie swears he saw Marilyn Monroe there once, but he also claims to have seen Batman climb the Revlon Building.

One of the stores we liked best was Frederick's of Hollywood. They sold lady's underwear, the kind called lingerie. Once, hoping to see more, I stuck my head inside the door. The manager grabbed me by the belt and hustled me outside.

"Come back when you're eighteen, sonny," he said.

Crank loved that one. He kept saying it for days, laughing and slapping his leg.

Sometimes as we walked, I would stare at my reflection in a store window and wonder what I was doing there. Not just in Hollywood, but with Crank, Arnie, and Oz. I was a plain sort of person, with straight brown hair and a face you wouldn't remember. I wasn't too short or too tall, too fat or too thin. Even my name was plain. It was Paul Smith. How did I end up with these guys? To me, they always seemed bigger than life, or at least bigger than mine.

We had met the year before, waiting for the school bus on the first day of seventh grade. I had noticed Arnie off to one side, nervously reading a science fiction magazine called *Astounding*. When the bus came, Arnie refused to get on, swearing he had seen someone called Dr. Death staring at him through the window. Crank, in line behind Arnie, tried to shove him onto the bus. Oz blocked the way, starting a sit-down strike in the doorway. Crank yelled at Oz. Oz yelled at Crank. Just as things were heating up, I noticed that Crank was carrying *Galaxy*, another science fiction magazine. I asked him about it, Arnie joined in, and the next thing I knew, the four of us were sitting together on the bus, thumbing through the magazines and describing our favorite monsters.

Near Frederick's of Hollywood was a newsstand that had papers from all over the world, plus every magazine you could think of. That day, as usual, we stopped to browse. Arnie, Crank, and I headed for the science fiction section. Oz picked up the *Hollywood Reporter*. His father was in the movie business, and I'd seen the magazine lying around their house. Oz flipped through it, and suddenly, toward the back, he stopped and stared.

"I don't believe it."

"What?" I asked, glancing up at him.

"It's amazing! It's incredible!"

"Will you just tell us?" said Crank.

Oz balanced the magazine on the tips of his fingers, the way you might hold a precious relic. "It says here that next week, they'll start filming a new horror movie. It's called *Invasion of the Body Snatchers*."

"What's so amazing about that?" I asked.

"You don't get it," said Oz. "The amazing thing isn't what they're filming. It's where."

"So, where is it?" asked Arnie.

"Gentlemen," said Oz, "*Invasion of the Body Snatchers* will be filmed in our hometown, Sierra Madre."

2 · GET PEZ!

You have to understand, nothing happens in Sierra Madre.

It's a nice little town, with the emphasis on *little*. You could walk from one end to the other in a half hour, except that every few minutes you'd be stopped by someone wanting to talk—your teacher, the mailman, the librarian, your neighbor's kid sister, your best friend's second cousin once removed. We talk a lot in Sierra Madre, because there's not much else to do.

Our idea of a big event is the Wistaria Festival. For one week every March, old Mrs. Lambert opens up her backyard to the public, so people can visit her famous wistaria vine. She claims it's the biggest plant in the world, but to me it just looks like a vine. Don't tell the store owners though. Up and down Baldwin Avenue, our main street, they hold special sales to celebrate the festival.

I live two blocks from Baldwin on a street called Mountain Trail, in a house that used to be a blacksmith's shop. Our town is tucked up against the San Gabriel Mountains, and at the top of my street is a path winding up to one of the highest peaks, Mount Wilson, where there's a famous observatory and telescope. My friends and I have hiked up to see it a few times. The telescope was hauled, piece by piece, on the backs of mules whose shoes were made right in my house. The year was 1908, when no one had ever heard of a flying saucer.

Oz lives around the corner from me and a few doors down, on Highland. I stopped by on Monday morning, the way I always do, so we could walk together to the school bus. On the way I passed Mr. Ward, who was trimming his hedge. He owns Ward's Jellies & Jams, a business he runs from a room over his garage.

He looked up and smiled. "Morning, Paul. Beautiful day."

"Yes, sir."

Watching him work, I wondered what Mr. Ward would say if he knew his town was about to be invaded by body snatchers.

I picked up Oz and we walked to the bus stop, on Baldwin. Arnie and Crank were waiting for us. Crank was hungry, so we went into Royal Drugs with him to buy a candy bar.

"Get PEZ!" Arnie told him.

"I hate PEZ," said Crank.

"But they're so cool," said Arnie.

Of course, Arnie didn't mean the candy. He was talking about the PEZ dispenser. It was plastic with a button on top.

When you pushed the button, candy popped out. I'd seen Arnie sit there for hours, dispensing PEZ.

The great thing was, there were different shapes on top of the dispensers. There was Santa Claus, Mickey Mouse, and a space trooper. At the back of the candy rack that day was a dispenser I'd never seen before. It had a monster on top.

Arnie was on it in a flash. He snagged it from the rack and waved it in Crank's face.

"You've got to buy this!" he said in that whiny little voice he used when he was excited. "I think it's a body snatcher!"

"How do you know?" asked Oz.

Arnie said, "It just looks like one."

Crank sighed. "All right. But I'm picking the flavor."

He got some PEZ from the rack, took the dispenser from Arnie, and headed to the counter, where the clerk put the items into a bag and rang them up. Mr. Rollins, the owner, was hanging a sign nearby.

"Big week, kids," he said. "The Wistaria Festival starts on Wednesday. We'll have special sales in all the stores."

"Mr. Rollins," I said, "it's just a vine."

He said, "Come on down. Tell your friends."

"Oh, we'll be here," said Oz. "That's the first day of filming."

"Filming?"

Oz pulled out the *Hollywood Reporter* he had bought at the newsstand. He showed Mr. Rollins the article. Mr. Rollins scanned it, then looked up, concerned.

"It says they'll be filming on the town square. That's right here."

"Isn't it great?" I said. "There'll be lights and cameras. They'll probably block off the street."

He said, "They can't do that. What about our customers? What about the sale?"

"Who cares?" said Oz. "Sierra Madre is going to be famous."

But Mr. Rollins wasn't listening. He asked the clerk to watch the store, then went next door to Perry's Stationery.

Meanwhile, Arnie took the bag from Crank and started loading PEZ into the dispenser.

"Hey, give it!" said Crank.

Clucking his tongue, Oz said, "Poor Eugene. Did somebody take his candy?"

Crank grabbed Oz by the front of his shirt. "Shut up! And don't call me Eugene."

Arnie took off down the sidewalk toward the bus stop, holding the dispenser high like a torch. Crank let go of Oz and lumbered after him.

"You little weasel!" he bellowed.

Oz watched them, straightening his shirt. "There's your next movie," he said. "Talk about a horror film."

"Drop!" said Mrs. Kramer.

Pushing back my chair, I dove beneath the desk. I crouched on the floor, knees to my chest, eyes shut tight, hands protecting my head the way they had taught us. I heard the hollow click of Mrs. Kramer's footsteps as she hurried to the windows and lowered the blinds. Then there was silence.

I waited for the bomb.

I imagined a Russian missile whistling in over the clouds and striking somewhere beyond the horizon. The ground would rock, and a mushroom cloud would appear over the trees, red and angry. A shock wave of superheated air and debris would speed toward us, destroying everything in its path.

Once a week, we had drop drills at school. It was up to each teacher to decide when. Suddenly, in the middle of a reading exercise or math problem, the teacher would whirl and yell, "Drop!" We didn't have time to think or plan. We just threw ourselves to the floor. I always had the same thought.

Maybe this time it's not a drill. Maybe it's real. I waited for the explosion and the shock wave. I wondered how it felt to die.

"All right, kids, on your feet," said Mrs. Kramer. "Let's get back to work." She raised the blinds, then strode to the front of the class.

It was third period at Wilson Junior High School, and I was in class with Arnie, Crank, and Oz. Mrs. Kramer taught social studies, or at least her version of it, which was kind of like our horror movies. There were the good guys, the Americans. There were the bad guys, the Russians. There was even a monster, though she never said it that way. It was the bomb.

She told us how the United States had developed the atomic bomb during World War II to stop the Germans. Scientists were brought to Los Alamos, a secret base in New Mexico, and put to work on a special program called the Manhattan Project. There was a theory that if you split an atom, incredible amounts of energy would be released, causing an explosion bigger than anything the world had ever seen.

After three years of work, the scientists were ready to test their theory. They set off the first atomic bomb in the middle of the desert. There was a roar and a blinding flash. In an instant, everything was vaporized—the soil, the sand, the cactus, the birds. All of it went billowing upward, forming a huge dome and then a mushroom cloud ten miles high. Even the scientists were amazed by the power of the explosion.

By then Germany had surrendered, but Japan was still fighting. It looked as if the only way to stop them was to invade Japan—or use the bomb. So we dropped atomic bombs on two of their cities, Hiroshima and Nagasaki. Hundreds of thousands of people were killed. Mrs. Kramer showed us pictures of Hiroshima after the bomb. For miles around where it had hit, nothing was left. There were no buildings. There were no bodies. They were gone. A few days later, Japan surrendered.

"World War Two is over," said Mrs. Kramer, pacing back and forth at the front of the class. "But now we're in another war, a cold war. It's us against the Russians, democracy versus communism. Both sides have the bomb. Why do you think we have drop drills? If some general in Moscow gets an itchy finger, it could be like Hiroshima all over again."

I didn't say anything, but I couldn't help wondering, *If it's like Hiroshima, what good are drop drills?* Whether I was sitting at my desk or crouched underneath, I would end up the same way. Dust. Vapor. Atomic particles.

Arnie raised his hand. "Do you think they'd bomb Sierra Madre?"

There was nervous laughter.

Mrs. Kramer said, "How many of your parents are in the defense industry?"

I raised my hand, along with six or seven other people.

"Where does your father work, Paul?" she asked.

"At Lockheed," I said. It was an aircraft company in Los Angeles.

"What does he do there?"

I realized I didn't know the answer. I shrugged. "Make planes, I guess."

A few people laughed. It made me mad, first at them, then at my father. I'd lived with him for thirteen years and had no idea what his job was. How can you be so close to someone and know so little about him?

Mrs. Kramer said, "A lot of the defense industry is based in Los Angeles. The Russians know that. It would be a target."

"But Los Angeles is ten miles away," said Arnie.

Crank snorted. "Haven't you heard of the hydrogen bomb?"

Arnie shrugged. "It's like an atomic bomb, right?"

"Yeah, but a hundred times stronger," said Crank. "The Russians have it too."

Arnie looked at Mrs. Kramer. She nodded grimly.

"The Russians have the H-bomb," she said. "If they bomb Los Angeles, Sierra Madre will fall."

Sierra Madre will fall. The way she said it scared me, but it also made me proud. Sierra Madre was important. It could be a battleground, like Normandy or Iwo Jima.

Mrs. Kramer started pacing again. "It's a war, kids. We're soldiers, all of us. Our job is to fight communism wherever we find it."

"Like at school?" asked a girl in the front row.

"Hey," said a boy behind her, "I saw a Communist in the cafeteria. He was drinking pink lemonade."

"It's not a joke," said Mrs. Kramer. She told us about some of the people who were fighting communism. Senator Joseph McCarthy had held hearings in Congress. J. Edgar Hoover, head of the FBI, was leading investigations.

"We have to be on guard, all of us," she said. "We need to look around and see what's going on. If we don't, do you know what happens?"

We glanced at each other. No one said a word.

"What happens," Mrs. Kramer said, "is this."

She took a sheet of paper from her briefcase, unfolded it, and held it up for us to see. Being a fan of horror movies, I expected some kind of monster, maybe a mutant sea creature or a radioactive zombie. Instead, I saw a man with short hair and a pleasant face wearing a coat, tie, and glasses. He looked like someone who could live next door, the kind of person who might cut his grass on Saturdays and contribute money to the school band.

"Who is he?" someone asked.

Mrs. Kramer said, "Ladies and gentlemen, meet Klaus Fuchs. He was one of the scientists working on the A-bomb at Los Alamos. He was also a Russian spy. Everything he knew, he passed along to them. Because of Klaus Fuchs, the Russians have the bomb. And we have drop drills. Anytime, without warning, you and I could be turned to cinders."

I looked at Arnie, Crank, and Oz. All I saw was a pile of ashes.

"Our enemies are all around," said Mrs. Kramer. "They're here. They're real. Watch out for them. It's everybody's job."

After class, we walked to our lockers. I had noticed Oz fidgeting while Mrs. Kramer talked, and I asked him about it.

Oz shook his head. "It's nothing."

"He's scared," said Crank. "Look at him. He's afraid we'll be vaporized."

"Shut up, will you?" said Oz.

Crank stepped in front of Oz, blocking his path. "You got a problem?"

Oz dropped his gaze for a moment, then looked back up, defiant. "My grandfather was one."

"One what?" asked Arnie.

"A Communist."

We stared at him. He might as well have told us his family came from Mars.

Oz said, "He was a labor organizer. He always said the one group that wasn't afraid to fight for workers was the Communist Party."

"But they're the enemy," said Arnie.

Crank peered at Oz. "Your grandfather was a commie?"

"Don't call him that," said Oz.

Crank grinned. "What's wrong, Feldman? Can't stand the truth?"

"He was a good man."

"He was a traitor," said Crank.

Oz went barreling into him headfirst, pounding Crank's chest with his fists, like a chihuahua attacking a doberman. I wanted to stop them but didn't know what to do. As I looked on, Crank fended him off easily, then grabbed his arm and twisted it behind him.

I said, "Come on, guys, cut it out."

"Your grandfather was a traitor," Crank declared. "Say it."

"No!" gasped Oz.

"Say it or I'll break your arm."

"Hey!" Mr. Mullen, the football coach, came hurrying over. Crank let go of Oz. "What's going on here?" asked Mr. Mullen.

We didn't answer.

He glared at us. "No fighting. I catch you again, you're suspended. Got it?"

Oz and Crank nodded. Mr. Mullen shot them another look, then headed off.

Crank went around for the rest of the day with a smirk on his face. Oz was angry but silent. Arnie was nervous.

I didn't know what to think. I just wanted them to be friends. I wanted them to smile and say everything was fine. It was fine, wasn't it?

My father watches a lot of TV. We were the first family on the block to get one. My father set it up in the middle of the living room and bought a reclining chair to put in front of it—you know, the big overstuffed kind where you pull a lever on the side to make the headrest go back and the foot rest pop up.

It was the same every night. He would finish his dinner, then turn on the TV, lean back in his recliner, and stare at whatever was on. He was a big man, with broad shoulders and a worried expression. He was balding in front. His forehead was covered with wrinkles, and every year it got wider, as if the wrinkles were spreading, gradually taking over his face.

My mother would wash the dishes, then go into the living room and sit next to him. Of course, there was only one recliner, so she would pull up a chair from the dining room. She was a small thin woman with sharp features and eyes that constantly checked the room, looking for problems.

And there were plenty of them, usually caused by my sister, Lulu. Lulu was eight years old. She liked to buzz around the room, making trouble and noise. My father would frown, and my mother would say, "Shush, Lulu." We heard it so often, one of the neighbor kids thought that was her name. Shush Lulu.

Me, I tried to stay out of sight. It was better that way. Besides, I didn't like TV as much as they did. Sure, it was great having Gene Autry and Elmer Fudd piped into your living room. But they were black-and-white and barely six inches tall. When you've been to a movie theater, dodging thirty-foot monsters and wading through pools of bright red blood, the world inside a TV seems kind of puny.

So I tended to stay in my room, reading *Amazing Stories*. But that night was different. I went out into the living room, took a deep breath, and approached my father.

"What do you do at work?" I asked. The question had been bothering me all day.

He gazed at the TV. "You wouldn't understand."

"Maybe I would."

My mother nudged me. There was a warning in her eyes. For once, I ignored it. My heart was racing.

"All my friends know what their parents do," I told him.

"Drop it," he said.

"Why can't you tell me?" I asked.

"I said drop it."

"Why? I want to know. You're my father."

That's when he gave me the Look. It happened whenever people asked about his job. For some reason it made him mad. The Look was like an alien death ray, only worse. It burned, but it was cold as ice. It made you want to shrivel up and die. There were no words. There was only silence and anger.

That night I had the dream again. Something was chasing me. It was big and dark. I couldn't quite make it out. Sometimes it was off in the distance. Other times it was right on top of me, breathing down my neck.

Once I told my mother about the dream. She shivered and pulled me close. She was scared too. Maybe everybody is. They pretend things are fine, but they're not. The Russians could swoop out of the sky and take over. They could drop a bomb, and the world would explode. Just blow up any minute.

The world is a dangerous place, full of people and things that can hurt you. That's what I like about horror movies— at least they show it. The monsters may have zippers, but there really are monsters. They're in the backyard. They're all around.

3 · POD PEOPLE

"MR. BOWER, CAN'T YOU HURRY?" I ASKED THE BUS DRIVER.

"Sorry, Paul, I'm doing the best I can."

It was Wednesday afternoon, and the school bus was stuck in traffic. All we could do was wait, while just a few miles away, body snatchers were invading Sierra Madre.

Early that morning, Oz and I had arrived downtown an hour before the school bus, hoping to catch sight of the movie crew. We hadn't been disappointed. There must have been a hundred people there. After blocking off Baldwin Avenue with sawhorses and yellow tape, they had set up camera positions on the roof of the Sierra Madre Hotel. They milled around, drinking coffee and eyeing the sun.

Off to one side, Mr. Rollins and a group of other store owners were arguing with one of the movie people. The man had silver hair, a gray sport coat, a dark tie, and black slacks with a perfect crease.

I looked around and saw Mrs. Peterson, a tall red-haired

woman who ran Mama Pete's Nursery School just a few blocks away. I had spent my days there during the war, while my father had fought in Europe and my mother had worked at a munitions plant. It had been over ten years since Mrs. Peterson had taken care of me, but I still remembered her knowing eyes and quick smile. Today she had a camera and was taking some home movies. Lowering the camera, she spotted us.

"Hello, boys," she said. "Isn't it exciting?"

"Who's the man talking to Mr. Rollins?" I asked.

"That's Walter Wanger. They say he's the producer, the one in charge."

"Mr. Rollins sure looks mad," I said.

Mrs. Peterson shook her head. "Poor, silly Mr. Rollins. He and his friends think the movie will hurt their business. If they had half a brain, they'd realize it was the best thing that could have happened. It's seven in the morning, and already a crowd's starting to gather. Not to mention the movie people."

Glancing around, she nodded toward a man and woman standing off to the side, talking and going over the script.

"See those two? Somebody told me they're the stars, Kevin McCarthy and Dana Wynter."

Movie stars in Sierra Madre! Just imagining it gave me goose bumps. I was still thinking about it that afternoon, stuck in traffic on the school bus.

Arnie fidgeted in his seat. "Can't we go faster? By the time we get there, they'll be done filming."

"Stop whining," said Crank. He gave Arnie a shove, sending him sprawling in the aisle.

Oz, sitting with me in the seat behind them, helped Arnie to his feet and glared at Crank. "Why are you such a jerk?"

"At least I'm not a commie jerk," said Crank.

Oz lunged at him. I stepped in and broke it up. Since their fight after Mrs. Kramer's class, I'd been doing a lot of that. It was as if we were the crew of a spaceship, under attack by aliens and starting to fight among ourselves. The ship had been damaged. It was whirling in space, faster and faster, ready to fly apart, and I was the only one who could stop it. It was all up to me.

Arnie, who had moved to the window, called out, "Hey, I see something. There are flashing lights."

We crowded in next to him and gazed out the window. Two police cars were parked sideways in the street, with their red lights turned on. Beyond them was a truck that had apparently spilled its load. One of the officers was directing traffic, while the other helped the truck driver clean up.

Mr. Bowers, directed by the officer, guided his bus carefully around the truck. As we drove past, Oz eyed the spill.

"What are those things?" he asked.

I looked at the objects that were scattered across the street. About five feet long, green, and scaly, they were pointed on the ends and thick and round in the middle.

"They look like giant seeds," said Arnie.

"Yeah, sure," said Crank.

"Well," said Arnie, "what else would they be?"

Crank didn't answer. None of us did.

Once we got around the truck, the bus sped up, and we were downtown in no time. We grabbed our books and hurried off the bus.

"You think they'll still be filming?" I asked Oz.

"I hope so," he said.

We shouldn't have worried. The film crew was there, along with a crowd of people. Circulating among them was Mr. Rollins, selling candy and sunglasses. The crew was checking the cameras, adjusting the lights, eating snacks. Mostly, though, they were standing around. I wondered what they were waiting for.

A few minutes later, they perked up. A man pointed. "It's here," he shouted. "Let's go, people."

I followed his gesture. Down the street, approaching the blocked-off intersection, was the truck that had spilled its load in the street. Next to me, a woman wearing coveralls and a baseball cap picked up one end of a sawhorse and swung it around to unblock the street. The truck pulled in and stopped right in front of us.

I asked the woman, "What's the truck for?"

"It's in the movie," she said.

Arnie checked the back of the truck. The green things were stacked up inside. "What are those?" he asked.

"Seedpods," she told him.

Arnie looked at us and grinned. "Told you so."

Crank said, "Those are seeds? What do they grow into?"

"Body snatchers," said the woman.

She picked up one of the seedpods and, without giving Arnie time to think, tossed it to him. He screamed and jumped back. The pod clattered to the street with a hollow sound. Crank stepped over to inspect it.

"It's plastic," he said.

"Are you sure?" asked the woman. "I heard it came from outer space. I heard it grows in your basement, and in the middle of the night, when you fall asleep, it pops open. Inside, there's an alien that takes your place. It looks and acts just like you. Except it has no soul."

"A pod person," I said. "A body snatcher."

"Exactly," she said.

Arnie looked back and forth between us. "You guys are kidding, right?"

The woman gazed at him. "Don't fall asleep," she said. "Of course, eventually we all do."

She walked off. Maybe it was my imagination, but I thought there was a strange sort of stiffness in the way she walked.

"Okay, people, let's clear the area. You're in the shot."

It was the man who had spotted the truck a few minutes earlier. He moved us out of the street, then motioned to the camera operator on top of the hotel. A few minutes later, another man called out through a bullhorn, "Quiet, please. All right, here we go. Speed. Action."

They were filming at the intersection of Baldwin Avenue and Sierra Madre Boulevard. Near the intersection, a diagonal street connected the two roads, cutting off a triangular area that had been made into a tiny park, bounded by sidewalks, with grass and a tree in the middle. It was called Kersting Court.

As the scene began, the truck pulled up next to Kersting Court, along with two other trucks loaded with seedpods. As soon as the trucks parked, people began moving toward them. I recognized some of the people who had been in the crowd. I hadn't remembered seeing them around town before, and now I knew why. They were actors. There were dozens of them, all walking purposefully to the trucks. The strange thing was that no one spoke. They just lined up behind the trucks, where each of them received a seedpod to take out into the world.

That wasn't the only thing that was strange. Their motions were odd and mechanical, like those of the woman in the coveralls. Their expressions were blank. They didn't look around. They just walked away stiffly, holding the seedpods. It appeared to be a normal town—my town—but something awful was happening.

"Cut! Let's try another one."

The man with the bullhorn called out instructions, and the actors returned the pods to the trucks. Over the next hour they tried the scene several more times. As they did, I began to notice one of the actors. She was blond, in her twenties, with full red lips and the most amazing eyes. She wore a yellow dress that swirled around her legs when she walked. I couldn't stop watching her.

I elbowed Oz. "Did you notice that one?"

"Which one?"

"The beautiful one."

He said, "They're actors. They're all beautiful."

I pointed her out, and he smiled. "They'll be done in a minute. Why don't you talk to her?"

Arnie, who had been listening, burst out, "Are you crazy? She might be an alien."

"She's a babe," said Crank. "An alien babe."

"This is scary," said Arnie.

As we watched, the truck drivers started gathering up the pods. The crew folded up the tables, and the actors began to leave.

"They're finished," Oz told me. "Here's your big chance."

The woman walked toward us. Up close she didn't look like an alien. Her skin was soft and smooth. Her eyes were deep blue.

I stepped forward. "Excuse me."

She turned toward me. Her face lit up in a smile. "Yes?"

"I was just wondering. . . ." I had no idea what to say.

"He wants your autograph," said Oz.

"That's right," I said. "Can I have your autograph?"

"Me?" she said. "I'm just an extra."

"He thinks you're beautiful," said Oz.

I started to object, but the woman smiled again. Her eyes sparkled. I had always wondered what that expression meant, and now I knew.

"I've got a pen," said Arnie.

He reached into his pants pocket and took out a ballpoint he'd been using since the third grade. It was shaped like a rocket ship, with three buttons on the side. Depending on which button you pushed, it would write in red, green, or blue.

The woman didn't seem to mind. Taking the pen, she said, "I'd be happy to give you an autograph."

My hands shook as I tore a sheet of paper from my school notebook and handed it to her.

She asked, "What's your name?"

"Paul."

"Really? That's my brother's name."

Crank smirked. "Is he an alien too?"

I glared at Crank. The woman smiled, then looked back at me. "My brother's wonderful," she said. "In fact, you remind me of him."

She leaned down to sign the paper. Since she was an actress, I expected her to have fancy handwriting. Instead, she wrote in small neat letters at the top of the page.

To Paul,

Best wishes,

Laura Burke

She handed it back to me.

Arnie said, "Can I have one?"

Crank shifted from foot to foot. "Me too," he mumbled, embarrassed.

"Of course," she said. She signed their notebooks and turned to Oz. "How about you?"

"Want a milk shake?" he asked.

The woman laughed. "Are you asking me on a date?"

Arnie said, "Lady, he's only thirteen years old."

"Will you shut up?" said Crank.

Oz told her, "We like movies. I thought maybe you could tell us about this one."

She looked at her watch. "I'm meeting a friend in a few minutes, so I don't have time for a milk shake. But we can talk until he comes."

She handed the pen back to Arnie, who accepted it proudly. We introduced ourselves, and she told us we could call her Laura.

The breeze blew. There was a faint scent of lavender. Laura turned to Oz and said, "Now, what did you want to know?"

4 · HELLO, LAURA

"How long have you been in the movies?" I asked.

Laura glanced around. "Can I tell you a secret? This is my first one."

"Really?"

"Those are the first autographs I've ever signed. I guess that makes you my first fans."

"But you're so good," I said.

Crank snorted. "All we've seen her do is walk. I mean, no offense."

She chuckled. "That's true. But I'll be doing more. When they hired me, they said I looked like one of the stars, Carolyn Jones. They asked me to be her double."

Oz saw the confusion in my face. "Sometimes when they set up a shot," he said, "the star is a long way off or looking in the other direction so you can't see their face. That's when a double stands in, so the star doesn't have to be there."

Laura said, "The other stars haven't been using doubles,

but Carolyn Jones wanted one. It means I get more time with the director and producer."

"Aren't you scared?" Arnie asked her.

"No, they're nice people."

"I'm talking about the others," said Arnie. He jerked his head toward a crowd of extras. "If you ask me, those people are acting pretty strange."

She laughed. "Well, of course they are. They're aliens. You boys know the story, don't you?"

"Not really," I said.

Reaching into her purse, she pulled out a couple of rolled-up magazines. "The movie's based on a short story that was in two issues of *Colliers*."

She unrolled the magazines and handed them to me. I opened the first one to a marked page. A title blazed across the top.

The Body Snatchers

by Jack Finney

Beneath the title was a drawing of a man and woman running from a crowd of zombies.

"Wow," I said.

"I don't need these magazines anymore," said Laura. "Would you like to borrow them?"

"Could I?"

Arnie squawked, "Hey, how come he gets them?"

"Shut up," said Crank.

Before Arnie could answer, there was a voice behind us. "Hello, Laura."

We turned around and saw one of the other actors. He was a tall thin man a few years younger than Laura, with brown hair cut short, military style. The man was smiling, but his eyes darted nervously around the area. In his hand he held a small notebook.

He edged us aside and took Laura's hand, kissing her on the cheek. Eyeing us, he asked her, "Who are they?"

"They're my friends," she said.

As we introduced ourselves, I tried my best not to hate him. It didn't work.

"Boys," said Laura, "this is Darryl Gibbons. Darryl's been helping me with my acting."

I thought, *Yeah, I'll bet.*

"I've made a study of acting," said Darryl. "You know, little things that I've learned. I keep them in this notebook."

"Really?" said Oz. "Can I see it?"

Darryl chuckled. "It's over your head. Technical stuff. Acting's not as easy as it looks."

He turned to Laura. "Ready to go?"

"Sure," she said.

I was still holding Laura's magazines. "How do I get these back to you?" I asked her.

"Oh, we're not done shooting. We'll be here tomorrow.

In fact . . ." She pulled out a folded sheet of paper and handed it to me. "That's the shooting schedule, in case you're interested."

"Don't you need this?" I asked.

"You keep it," she said. "I'll get another one."

She smiled at Darryl, put her arm in his, and the two of them walked off.

"I don't like that guy," I said.

Crank grinned. "What's wrong? You jealous?"

"It's more than that," said Oz. "There's something strange about him."

Arnie said, "Cut it out, guys. You're scaring me."

Remembering the schedule, I unfolded it, and the others gathered around to look.

"Wow," said Oz, "they're shooting the whole movie in three weeks. That's quick."

It was true. The schedule showed two more days of filming in Sierra Madre, then a week in the San Fernando Valley and a final week in Hollywood and Griffith Park.

"You think we could go?" I said.

Crank stared at me. "To all of them?"

"Wouldn't it be great?" said Arnie. "We could see the whole movie. We could find out what happens to the pods."

"That's crazy," said Crank. "We've got school."

I could see Oz thinking. "The days in Sierra Madre should be fine, since we can come when school's over. Crank's right about next week, though. With classes during the day, we'd never make it to the San Fernando Valley. But the week after that . . ."

"Vacation!" I said. "That's spring break."

I imagined the four of us on a movie set somewhere in Hollywood. Oz was giving advice to the director. Arnie ran around the pod people, dispensing PEZ. Crank was right behind him, yelling. I was there too. So was Laura.

Closing my eyes, I pictured her again. I imagined the two of us talking, our shoulders touching. We didn't have to be like my mother and father, afraid to say anything, afraid to laugh or move. We could be different, I was sure of it.

In my mind, Laura smiled and took my hand. As she did, I saw another figure over her shoulder, his face in shadow. It was Darryl Gibbons.

"Pass the beans."

I looked at my father, surprised. He had spoken. He had used actual words.

It was more than we usually got. When dinner started he would drift in from the other room, sit down, and lean over the plate, his eyes hidden. He ate, sort of. It was more like refueling, the way the planes did at Lockheed Aircraft.

"Give your father the beans, Paul," said my mother.

"Yeah, Paul, pass the beans," said Lulu. She liked to make sure I did as I was told.

I shot her a look, then passed the beans to my father and went back to my reading. As soon as I'd arrived home after the filming that day, I had gone to my room and pulled out the magazines Laura had lent me. I had read for an hour or so, and when my mother called me to dinner I'd stuck a magazine in my science book and pretended to study while I ate.

The story was about a small-town doctor, Miles Bennell, who began to hear strange stories from his patients. Some of them claimed that friends or family members were impostors. Then, a few days later, those same patients would come back and tell him not to worry, that it was all a misunderstanding.

One night, Miles received a call from his friend Jack, who had discovered a body at his house. Miles and his girlfriend, Becky Driscoll, discovered that bodies like the one Jack had found had grown from giant seedpods and were hidden in basements all over town. When their hosts fell asleep, the bodies would come to life and replace them.

Miles and Becky, fighting off sleep, were chased by the pod people through town and into the hills, where they hid in a cave and made plans to escape and tell the world.

"Hey," said Lulu, "how come Paul gets to read at the table?"

"You really shouldn't," my mother told me.

"I have a science test tomorrow. It's important."

Lulu leaned over to look at the book. I tried to cover it up, but it was too late.

"Hey," she said, "he has a magazine in that book!"

I glared at her. "Thanks a lot."

My father glanced up from his plate, reached over, and took the magazine. I watched nervously as he looked over the story.

"Science fiction?" he grunted.

I nodded. "Want to read it?"

"No, thanks," he said, handing it back. "I get enough science fiction at work."

I perked up. "At work? Really?"

He shook his head and leaned over his plate. I started to ask what he meant but decided not to. I was afraid I'd get the Look.

"Are there monsters in that story?" asked Lulu.

I shrugged. "Sort of."

"You've got monsters on the brain," she said.

"At least I have a brain."

Lulu whirled in her chair and faced my mother. "Did you hear that?"

"Don't worry, dear. He's putting the magazine away. Aren't you, Paul?"

I sighed. "Yeah, I guess."

When I set it aside, my mother noticed the name. "*Colliers Magazine?* Where did you get that?"

"From a friend. They're making the story into a movie."

I wanted to tell her about the filming, maybe even about Laura. But I was afraid that if I said something, she'd tell me not to go.

She took a sip of coffee, watching me over the brim of her cup. "What is it about those movies?" she asked. "Why do you like them so much?"

How could I explain it to her? I liked them because they scared me. They showed my world. They fit my dreams. They told the truth.

But it was more than that. I looked around the room. There was no color, no life. I lived in a black-and-white house. All the things in it were shades of gray—our furniture, our clothes, our faces, our words. We barely spoke. Sometimes it seemed that we barely moved.

Horror movies were different. People shouted. They screamed. They stampeded, chased by creatures with three heads. The creatures attacked, and there was blood. The blood was red. The sky was purple. The monsters were sickly green.

It was the same reason I'd been drawn to my friends. Their lives were exciting. Their families were loud. Things happened. People told you what was on their minds. They fought, then made up. Even their food was colorful. While we ate white bread and potatoes, they served spaghetti, lasagna, eggplant, chopped liver. It smelled. It throbbed. It called out to you, then jumped off the plate and grabbed you.

I didn't spend much time at home. Usually I was with my friends. I kept expecting my mother to say something about it, but she didn't. Sometimes I think she understood. Other times, like that night after dinner, I watched her sitting beside my father, staring at the TV, and I wondered.

What were they thinking? What were they feeling? Somewhere deep down inside, were they laughing? Did they cry? Did they ever have a broken heart?

Maybe not. Maybe, like the pod people, they didn't feel a thing.

5 · THE COFFIN

MILES AND BECKY WERE RUNNING FOR THEIR LIVES.

It was a beautiful day in Sierra Madre. The stores were open. The flowers were blooming. Cars were parked neatly along the curb. Maybe a little too neatly.

The drivers, more than a hundred of them, were sprinting up Baldwin Avenue, their eyes blank, trying to catch the only two humans left in town. Miles and Becky looked over their shoulders, then headed for the hills.

"Cut! Okay, people, let's try it again."

It was late Thursday afternoon. Arnie, Crank, Oz, and I had hurried downtown after school, wondering what scenes we had missed. As it turned out, we hadn't missed any, because it had taken most of the day to set up the big chase. Several blocks of Baldwin Avenue had had to be cleared out, including all the cameras and scaffolding from the previous day, as well as all the real people in town, who were looking phonier by the minute. We stood with a group of them behind the camera, which had been set up at the Shell station.

During a break in the action, a team of assistants herded the extras back down Baldwin, while Kevin McCarthy and Dana Wynter took a breather, wiping off perspiration and sipping cool drinks.

"Where's your girlfriend?" Oz asked me.

I shrugged, pretending I didn't know.

Crank grinned. "Don't let him fool you. He's been watching her from the minute we got here."

He was right, though I wouldn't have admitted it. Before the scene began I had spotted Laura among the extras, checking her makeup and talking to Darryl. I wondered what she was telling him.

When the scene started I watched them run up the street, side by side. She was beautiful when she ran. She was beautiful, period.

The director had them do the scene a couple of more times, then dismissed all of them for the day. As the crew cleaned up and the people from town drifted back onto Baldwin Avenue, I noticed Laura at the Shell station, talking with two men. I edged closer, trying to hear what they were saying. My friends edged along with me.

Suddenly Laura glanced up and noticed us. Appearing relieved, she motioned us over.

"Boys," said Laura, "I'd like you to meet someone. This is the director, Don Siegel. Don, these are friends of mine."

He was a man of medium height, well tanned, with a

rugged face and a thin mustache. He wore a wrinkled hat and a work shirt. As he looked us over, we shook his hand and told him our names.

Arnie blurted, "We love horror movies. This is so cool."

Oz said, "I like your work, Mr. Siegel. I thought *Riot in Cell Block Eleven* was a small masterpiece."

Siegel's eyebrows shot up. "Oh, really?"

"Yes, sir. Your use of dramatic lighting and camera angles was brilliant."

I stared at Oz. Maybe he really was getting information from aliens.

Oz held out his hand. "It's an honor to meet you, sir. I'm Oscar Feldman."

Siegel shook his hand, studying him. "Feldman. That sounds familiar."

"Maybe you know his father," said Arnie. "He's in the movie business."

"Of course!" said Siegel. "Maury Feldman, one of the best sound editors in Hollywood."

Oz shifted uncomfortably. "Thank you, sir."

"What's Maury doing these days?"

"He's . . . between jobs."

Crank snorted. Oz glared at him.

Laura said, "Boys, Don and I were just discussing something you may be able to help us with."

Siegel looked at her in surprise.

"The body cast," she explained. "I told you, I'm

claustrophobic. It scares me to be shut into a small space. Maybe they could come with me."

"What about your friend?" Siegel asked her.

Her face reddened. "Darryl? He promised he would stay with me, then skipped out at the last minute. Please, Don? Let them come. I really don't want to do it alone."

I had barely noticed the other man with them, but now he spoke up. "You won't be alone, Miss Burke. I'll be there."

He was a tall thin man with thick glasses and an intense stare. He gazed at her, jingling coins in his pockets. Laura glanced nervously at him, then back at Siegel.

"Please?" she said.

I didn't like the thought of Laura alone with the tall man. Obviously, she didn't either. I said, "We'd like to help, Mr. Siegel. We won't be any trouble, I promise."

Siegel studied me. He nodded his head toward the tall man.

"You know who that is?" asked Siegel.

"No," I said.

"He may be the most important person on the set—the production designer, Ted Haworth."

"What's a production designer?" asked Arnie.

Siegel nodded toward Oz. "Tell them."

Oz said, "That's the person who gives the film its overall look. He's in charge of the sets and props and costumes—anything you see on camera."

"Like the pods," said Siegel. "What do you think of those?"

"They give me the willies," said Arnie.

Laura shivered. "Me, too."

Haworth gazed at Laura, stricken. "You don't like them?"

"They're creepy," said Laura. "I don't even want to touch them."

Crank snorted. "Come on, they're just plastic. If you ask me, this whole thing about pod people is stupid."

"Don't be so sure," said Siegel. "Lots of people wake up in the morning, eat breakfast, and go about their day without smiling or thinking or noticing a thing. They're pod people. They're everywhere."

I glanced around nervously. "Like Miles?" I asked.

Siegel smiled. "You know the story."

"Yes, sir, I read it."

"I think this film can be special," he said, "but only if the production designer is creative. For instance, how do you show a person growing out of a seedpod? The person has to look real, but half-formed, like a sketch."

I looked at Oz. He shrugged.

"Tell them, Ted," said Siegel.

Haworth took off his glasses and used a handkerchief to clean them. Without the glasses, his eyes seemed small and pale.

"First," he said, "you create a plaster cast of the person, then use it to make a full-size clay model. You spread liquid latex over the model, and when it dries you peel it off. The latex gives a perfect likeness of the person, only smoother."

"Pretty slick, huh?" said Siegel. "No pun intended."

Laura said, "Three of the four stars have already done theirs. The only one left is Carolyn Jones. Yesterday she said she didn't want to do it. So Don came to me."

"Because you're her double?" asked Oz.

"Smart boy," said Siegel. He turned to Haworth. "Let's do it, Ted. I need her likeness for the scene tomorrow. If she wants the boys there, fine."

He started to leave, then turned back to us. "Thanks for helping out, guys. You can come back tomorrow if you want. We've got one more day of shooting in Sierra Madre."

I thought of the schedule Laura had shown us. I didn't want tomorrow to be our last day. "What about after that?" I asked. "Can we see more of the filming?"

Siegel considered my question, then smiled. "Sure. Come anytime you want."

He turned to Oz. "When you see your dad, give him my best, huh?"

"Yes, sir," mumbled Oz.

Siegel left, and we followed Ted Haworth and Laura. Behind the Shell station, the production crew had set up a row of trailers. There was one for each of the stars and another for the production office. At the end of the row was an unmarked trailer. Haworth used a key to unlock the door and led us inside.

The room seemed familiar, but I couldn't think why. Then it hit me. I'd seen the place, or some version of it, in a dozen horror movies. It looked like the laboratory of a mad scientist. There were drills and lathes and gadgets. Off to one side was a Bunsen burner. Blueprints lay on a table, and on the floor was a stack of pods. In the middle of it all, surrounded by a tangle of wires and cords, was a box shaped like a coffin.

Haworth moved through the trailer, checking gauges and equipment, then turned to Laura. "Ready, Miss Burke?"

I noticed for the first time that she was carrying a canvas bag. Her hand shook, and she was blinking rapidly. I glanced at the box and remembered that she suffered from claustrophobia.

"What are you going to do?" I asked Haworth.

He smiled mysteriously. "You'll see." Nodding toward the rear of the trailer, he told Laura, "There's a dressing room in back."

She went into the room and shut the door. While she was gone, we watched Haworth open a closet and take out a large metal vat with handles on the sides. He lifted it onto a low table next to the box, then took out a big bag filled with powder and emptied it into the vat. He added water and stirred, making a gooey white mixture.

"What's that?" asked Crank.

"Plaster of paris," said Haworth. "It's a special kind that hardens quickly."

As he finished stirring, Laura came out of the dressing room. Everyone stopped. The trailer was silent. I must have been staring, because Oz poked me with his elbow. My jaw clanked back into place.

"Is this all right?" she asked Haworth nervously.

"Perfect," he said.

She wore a bathing suit. It was a black one-piece suit with simple lines, the kind I had seen dozens of times at the beach. But this time Laura was inside it.

"Well, then," said Haworth, "let's get started."

Laura set down her bag and glanced over at us. "Promise you won't leave?"

"Are you kidding?" I said. "I mean, of course not."

Stepping over to the box, Laura pulled on a bathing cap and tucked her hair inside it. Then she climbed into the box, lay on her back, and closed her eyes. Her lids quivered.

Haworth watched her. He moved to the table, grasped the handles of the vat, and tipped it over the box. The mixture poured out onto Laura, thick and white, gradually covering her body. She was being buried alive.

Arnie gasped. Oz stared.

"Cool," said Crank.

Haworth smiled grimly. "As the plaster hardens, it heats up. The body temperature makes it worse. Believe me, gentlemen, it's anything but cool."

I wanted to do something. I wanted to yell. I wanted to grab Laura's hand, run from the trailer, and take her to a place where she would be safe and we could be together. But I didn't do anything. I just watched.

Before long she was covered to the waist. Haworth adjusted the vat, and the mixture began to pour over her neck and shoulders. Laura was shaking now.

"Lie still," said Haworth in a low soothing voice. "We don't want to have to do this again."

She took a series of deep breaths and managed to stop shaking.

Haworth continued to pour. Soon the only thing showing was her face, floating on the surface like a mask.

I said, "You're not going to cover everything, are you?"

"Yes," he replied. "Oh, yes."

I started forward, but Oz grabbed my arm. I looked over at him. He shook his head.

Haworth opened a drawer and took out a straw. It had red stripes, like the kind you get at the Dairy Queen.

"Miss Burke," he said, "this is the part I told you about. I'm going to put a straw in your mouth. You can breathe through it. You'll be just fine."

Laura clenched her eyes and opened her mouth. Haworth put the straw in. I could hear her breathing in and out, in and out.

"Excellent," said Haworth.

Moving back to the vat, he tipped it again, and the mixture poured over her face. A moment later, the only thing showing was the straw.

I tried to imagine how she felt, unable to see or move. I asked Haworth, who said he had tested the process on himself with the help of an assistant.

He smiled. "I found it strangely peaceful. Hot, though. Terribly hot."

He touched the smooth white surface of the plaster. It was hard. He tapped it lightly with his knuckles.

"She's cooked," he said. Then he looked at me and added, "Figure of speech."

With a chisel, Haworth gently separated the box from the plaster, then used a screwdriver to undo hinges at the corners of the box. The boards came loose and he set them aside, leaving a hard white block.

There was a muffled sound, then a faint cry, as if from a long distance away. But I knew where it was coming from.

The block of plaster jiggled. The cry grew louder. I thought of Laura inside—trapped, trying to move, burning up.

"Let her out!" I said.

"Be patient," said Haworth.

"No!" I dropped to my knees. "Laura! We're here. We're coming." I turned to Haworth. "Do something!"

Picking up a hammer, he used it to tap the chisel all the way around the block of plaster, halfway between the top and bottom. He gave one last tap, and the top came loose. He carefully tipped it back, as if opening the lid of a sarcophagus.

A mummy came leaping out.

It was covered in white from head to toe, and it was screaming. It stomped around the room. Chunks of plaster fell off, breaking and turning to dust at its feet. The scream became a shriek, shrill and out of control, like the natives in *King Kong*, like the monster in *Bride of Frankenstein*. Finally it dropped to its knees, sobbing and rubbing its eyes. The tears washed plaster from its face, and I saw Laura.

I stepped over beside her. "It's okay," I said.

She whispered, "Hold me, please."

How could I say no?

6 · A COMMUNIST PLOT

"WHERE WERE YOU?" DEMANDED LAURA.

Darryl looked up. He sat at one of the fold-up tables provided for the actors, wearing neatly pressed slacks and a sport coat, writing in his notebook while the crew finished putting away their equipment.

"Sorry," he said. "Something came up."

"You said you would stay with me."

Darryl shrugged. "Looks like you had plenty of company." He glanced over at the four of us, then stared at me. "What happened to you?"

My clothes were covered with white powder from holding Laura. I didn't want to brush it off. Laura herself was clean, having showered and changed in the trailer. While we waited for her, we had watched Haworth carefully work on the plaster cast, revealing a perfect impression of Laura.

Laura glared at Darryl. "He was helping out, which is more than I can say for you. Sometimes you're a real pain, you know that?"

She started to leave, then turned back to us. "Thank you, boys. You're very sweet."

Darryl watched her stomp off. He shook his head. "Women." Rising from the table, he said, "See you around, guys." He walked off in the opposite direction.

Arnie noticed Darryl's notebook on the table and started to say something, but Oz stopped him. Oz picked up the notebook and opened it. As he thumbed through, his eyes narrowed.

A voice said, "What do you think you're doing?"

We turned and saw Darryl standing behind us. Something about him was different. His voice was low and menacing. His eyes were cold.

We backed away, all except Oz, who stood his ground.

"You said these notes were about acting," said Oz.

"That's right," said Darryl.

"You lied."

"Give me the notebook," said Darryl.

"There's information about people in the cast . . ."

"Give it to me."

". . . and about the director and producer."

Darryl's hand shot out. Before Oz knew what had happened, Darryl had snatched the notebook, closed it, and stuffed it into his pocket.

Oz studied him. "Who are you? What are you doing here?"

"I'm an actor," growled Darryl.

"Are you?"

Darryl turned and headed off.

"Tell us," Oz called after him.

Darryl kept going.

"We met Don Siegel today," said Oz. "He might like to hear about the notebook."

Darryl stopped and turned. His expression was blank, like the people in the movie.

He said, "Back off. Forget you saw anything. You have no idea what you're getting into."

"Well, guys," said Arnie, his voice shaking, "maybe we should go, huh?"

Crank, his eyes never leaving Darryl, grasped Arnie's arm and squeezed.

"Ow!" said Arnie.

"Shut up," said Crank.

Oz looked around at the rest of us, then back at Darryl. "All right. We won't tell Siegel. We won't tell anyone."

"Promise?" said Darryl.

"Promise," said Oz.

Darryl nodded. "Good."

"*If* you tell us the truth," said Oz.

Darryl's expression darkened. He took a quick step toward Oz, then thought better of it and stopped. The two of them stood nose to nose—well, nose to chest. Oz never flinched.

They stood that way for the longest time. Then Darryl reached inside his sport coat. I remembered gangsters I'd seen in movies, pulling guns from their coats and blowing away the cops.

I cringed. Crank froze. Arnie whimpered. Oz didn't budge. He watched as Darryl pulled out his wallet and flipped it open. Inside was a badge. It said *Federal Bureau of Investigation*.

FBI.

"Agent Darryl Gibbons," he said. "I'm running an investigation."

We gaped at him. Finally Crank said, "Can I see that?"

Darryl handed him the wallet. Crank inspected the badge, running his fingers over it. "Wow," he said.

The rest of us gathered around to look. Arnie murmured, "This is so cool."

Oz said, "If you're an actor, maybe this is just another part. The badge could be a prop."

"It could be," said Darryl. "But this isn't." He undid the top button of his shirt. Just below his collarbone was a wicked scar.

"I joined the bureau last year," he said. "I got this on my first assignment."

Oz watched as Darryl buttoned his shirt and put the wallet away. "I don't get it," said Oz. "Why would the FBI care about some horror movie?"

"Read the papers," said Darryl. "Communists are infiltrating Hollywood—the studios, the unions. Have you heard of HUAC?"

I hadn't. To me it sounded like some kind of vacuum cleaner.

Oz knew, of course. "Remember?" he told us. "Mrs. Kramer mentioned it. It's the House Un-American Activities Committee. It's a part of Congress. They investigate Communists."

Darryl nodded. "A few years back, the committee got interested in Hollywood. We believe they've just scratched the surface."

Oz said, "You think *Invasion of the Body Snatchers* is a Communist plot?"

"We're not sure," said Darryl. "We got a tip about it, and here I am."

"Spying on people," said Oz.

"Investigating," said Darryl. "Keeping the country safe."

Oz said, "You really believe that?"

Darryl's face reddened. He gestured angrily. "You see all this? The cars, the stores, the shoppers, the kids? Me and my buddies, we make it all possible. While you and your friends ride bikes and go to horror movies, we stand guard. We watch for the bad guys. We're the sentries at the door, making sure people like you can stay inside, twiddling your thumbs and picking your nose."

"At the same time?" said Oz. "Is that even possible?"

Crank said, "This isn't a joke. You heard him. It's national security."

"All right," said Darryl, "I've kept my end of the bargain. I told you the truth. Now I'm counting on you to keep yours. Don't tell anyone. This is top secret. Deal?"

"Deal," said Crank. He looked at the rest of us.

I wasn't sure what I thought, but I knew what a promise was.

"Deal," I said.

Oz shrugged. "Deal."

We looked at Arnie. He gave Darryl a nervous smile.

"Can I see your badge again?" he asked.

After Darryl left, we walked to Oz's place. Of our four houses, the Feldmans' was the one where we spent most of our time. It was comfortable, and there was always something to eat. We had tried Arnie's place for a while, but his mother kept coming through the room every five minutes, cleaning up after us. Crank's house was okay, if you didn't mind his little brother using your homework for paper airplanes or a Great Dane slobbering on you. We had even gone to my place once or twice, mostly for the TV, but Lulu had reported us to my dad, and that was the end of that.

On the way to Oz's house, we argued about Darryl and the FBI—what it meant and what we should do. As surprising as it all was, my mind was still on Laura. I saw her in the bathing suit. I saw her face floating in the coffin.

When we arrived, we grabbed some pretzels, opened our notebooks, and spread out on the floor to do verb conjugations for English class.

"Do aliens have homework?" asked Arnie.

Oz said, "I invade, you invade, he invades. . . ."

"*It* invades," corrected Arnie.

Crank snorted. "Here's one for you, PEZ boy. I quiver, you quiver, he quivers. . . ."

"Stop picking on him," said Oz.

"Make me."

As Oz started to get up, the hallway door opened and Maury Feldman walked in, wearing pajamas and carrying a half-empty bowl of cereal. His eyes were sunken, and his beard, usually neatly trimmed, stuck out in clumps.

He looked up and noticed us spread out on the floor. "Oh, I'm sorry," he said, turning back toward the door.

"It's all right," I said. "You okay, Mr. Feldman? I haven't seen you in a while."

He glanced at Oz, who fidgeted. There was an uncomfortable silence, and I jumped in.

"Hey, guess who we saw today? Don Siegel."

Mr. Feldman brightened. "Don Siegel? No kidding. I did some TV work with him a few years back."

"He told us to say hi."

Crank added, "He said you were good."

"The best," said Oz.

Crank glanced at Oz, then back at Mr. Feldman. "I hear you're between jobs."

Mr. Feldman dropped his gaze. Oz glared at Crank.

"So," I said quickly, "you're a sound editor? What's that like?"

Mr. Feldman murmured something.

Crank said, "What was that? I missed it."

"They stopped calling," said Mr. Feldman in a low voice.

"Why would they do that?" asked Crank.

Oz said, "You are such a jerk."

Reaching over, he gave Crank a shove. I moved between them.

"I'll tell you why," someone said.

We turned around and saw Bernice Feldman standing in the kitchen doorway. She was short, like Oz, with frizzy black hair that surrounded her face like a halo. When I'd first met her I had addressed her as Mrs. Feldman, and she had told me to call her Bernice. She had said it had something to do with equal rights.

"Bernice, please," said Mr. Feldman.

"They should know," Bernice told him. Turning to face us, she said, "In college Maury was part of a theater group. It was during the Depression, when times were hard. Some of the kids in the group took part in demonstrations, and one or two joined the Communist Party. Maury never did. But some people thought he did, and a few months ago they told the studios. That's when the phone stopped ringing. He was blacklisted."

"What does that mean?" asked Arnie.

Oz said, "The studios thought he was a Communist, so they wouldn't hire him."

"But he wasn't a Communist," I said.

"How do we know for sure?" asked Crank.

Bernice snapped, "Because I said so. Because he said so."

"They don't care about the truth," Oz explained. "Remember what Mrs. Kramer said about Senator McCarthy? He's holding hearings, trying to sniff out Communists. The studios are afraid. If they suspect someone, they put him on the blacklist."

"That's not fair," I said.

Bernice shook her head. "You've got a lot to learn."

She took Maury's cereal bowl and set it down. Gently holding his elbow, she led him into the hallway and closed the door behind them.

Oz turned back to his homework. Arnie didn't move. "You think there's an actual list?"

"Maybe," I said. "Maybe Darryl has it."

Arnie said, "But Darryl's with the FBI. He's one of the good guys, isn't he? Isn't he?"

No one answered.

7 · PLASTER AND LATEX

WE CALLED IT THE LIBERALMOBILE.

It was a 1952 Volvo, and Oz's mother drove it because Sweden had a good welfare system and universal health care. She used the car to donate household items to all her favorite organizations—the United Nations, the ACLU, the American Friends Service Committee. On the way, she sometimes gave us a ride.

"Where did you say this place is?" she asked.

Oz checked the shooting schedule. "Goya's Nursery, 600 Wilcox Street. I think it's right up here."

It was Friday, two days after seeing Oz's father. We hadn't said any more about what had happened, but the memory was there, like a cloud. It was in the car now. I wondered if the others could feel it.

After school that day, Bernice had been on her way to donate a lamp to the United Nations store, and we had talked her into dropping us off at the next movie location, a nursery in the hills above Sierra Madre. Oz sat in the front seat next to her, and the rest of us were wedged in behind them with the lamp.

Oz glanced at the lamp, then said to his mother, "Tell me again why we're giving this away?"

She stared at him.

From the backseat Arnie said, "Uh, can you watch the road please?"

"They'll find a use for it," said Bernice, swerving to avoid a parked car. "They always do."

"What about us?" said Oz. "Maybe we need it."

She snorted. "Don't be silly."

"We're always donating stuff," said Oz, "but it's not like we're rich."

Crank said, "Why give it to the United Nations? I heard it's a Communist front."

Suddenly the car was silent. I could see Bernice's jaw working. A row of trailers loomed up in front of us, parked along the curb. Bernice slammed on the brakes, stopping inches from the last one.

"Everybody out," she said.

It was just a narrow street up in the hills, but the place was overrun with movie people. A man hurried by carrying a bank of lights.

Crank turned to Bernice. "Hey, maybe they could use your lamp."

I shoved Crank out the door. "Thanks for the ride, Bernice."

Nearby, checking a clipboard, was Don Siegel. He saw us getting out and came over.

"Back for more?" he asked.

Oz held open the front door of the car. "Mr. Siegel, I'd like you to meet my mother, Bernice Feldman. Mom, this is the director, Don Siegel."

Bernice leaned across the seat. "You sure this is okay? I don't want the boys to bother you."

"They're fine," Siegel replied. "Your son knows more about movies than I do. Besides, I've worked with your husband. I owe him a favor."

"That's very nice," said Bernice. Eyeing us, she said, "All right then, boys. Call me if you need a ride home."

As she drove off, Oz turned to Siegel. "What did we miss?"

"Not much," he said. "Remember Ted Haworth's pod people? The ones he made from latex? Seems they weren't ready for their cue. He's been working on them all day."

I had a sudden vision of Laura the mummy jumping around Haworth's trailer, while Haworth leaned over the coffin, fiddling with the plaster cast.

"How do those things work?" I asked.

"The latex figures are like giant balloons," Siegel explained. "We put them inside the pods, and when we throw a switch, they fill up with air and pop out."

An assistant poked his head around a corner. "Hey, Don, Ted wants you."

"Can we come?" asked Oz.

"Sure," said Siegel. "Just don't get in the way." He disappeared into the nursery, and we followed.

The crew had set up in one of the greenhouses. Haworth was kneeling on the ground, working on what looked like a motor. Nearby were four of the giant seedpods.

Haworth looked up when we entered. His hair stuck out at odd angles, and his glasses were crooked.

"I think we're ready," Haworth told Siegel. "I fixed the hydraulics."

Siegel nodded and glanced around. "Okay, people," he called. "Vacation's over. Let's move."

A group of actors had been standing outside the greenhouse, drinking coffee from paper cups. When they heard Siegel, they set down the cups and approached.

Arnie elbowed Oz. "Hey, those are the stars, aren't they?"

Oz nodded. "That's Kevin McCarthy and Dana Wynter. The others are King Donovan and Carolyn Jones."

My ears perked up when he said Carolyn Jones. If she was there, maybe her stand-in was too. Sure enough, across an open area stood Laura, dressed identically to Jones. She was talking to Darryl.

We watched as Haworth placed seedpods around the floor of the greenhouse and covered the motor with ferns. He moved away, and Siegel set up the scene.

Finally Siegel said, "Let's make it a good one. Speed. Action."

The greenhouse was darkened. Miles entered. Light slanted through the open door. He searched for something, found it, and was about to leave when he heard a sound. Moving farther into the greenhouse to investigate, he came across a giant seedpod. It had opened up, and bubbles were oozing out. From inside, a hand popped free, then a foot and a head. Miles yelled for his friends, and they hurried to join him. As they watched in horror, a body took shape among the bubbles.

In that instant it became clear to them. The people in town were acting strange because they were aliens. They had come from pods like this one, placed all around town. Creatures that looked like humans grew inside, and when their hosts fell asleep, the creatures stepped out and replaced them.

Miles and Becky went inside to call the FBI, while their friends stayed in the greenhouse to watch. A cold breeze blew, and a face appeared among the bubbles. I gasped. It was Laura. She lay there with her eyes shut, every detail of her face perfect. Looking closer, I realized she was made of latex. It was the copy Ted Haworth had made the day before.

By the time Miles and Becky came back, three more pods had burst open, one for each of them. Miles, wild-eyed, grabbed a pitchfork and raised it over the creature that looked like Becky. He couldn't bring himself to kill it. Moving to his own likeness, he brought down the pitchfork again and again, then killed the other ones as well. When he stabbed Laura, it was all I could do to keep from crying out.

After the filming was over, Arnie said, "You think Laura's okay?"

"You idiot," said Crank. "That wasn't her." He slugged Arnie, like always, but I could see that he was shaken too.

"Let's go find her," I said. "You know, just to say hi."

As we left the greenhouse, we spotted Laura on the sidewalk in front of the nursery, arguing with Darryl. He said something, and she started to slap him. Stopping herself, she glared at him, then stomped off to her car and drove away.

Darryl watched her go, then pulled out his notebook and wrote something in it. When he looked up, we were standing in front of him.

"Is everything all right?" I asked.

He quickly closed the notebook and stuffed it into his coat pocket. "Just fine," he said, "except I'm starved. Is there someplace around here where I can get a burger?"

I wondered what he had written in the notebook. Maybe there was a way to find out.

"Sure," I said. "Great burgers. Homemade fries. There's only one catch. You have to take us with you."

"Yeah, right," he said.

I motioned to my friends. "Come on, guys. Let's go."

As we started to leave, he called, "Hey, what about the burgers?"

"They're not that good," I said.

A moment later he caught up with us.

"Do they have ice cream?" he asked.

It turns out that even FBI agents have weaknesses. In Darryl's case, it was ice cream.

We agreed to take him to D's Café and Malt Shop on Baldwin Avenue, just up the street from where the pod people had chased Miles and Becky the day before. When we climbed into his black Plymouth sedan, we knew for sure he was an FBI agent, not an actor. The car was newly waxed, and the interior was immaculate. He parked it at the curb, and we went inside to our favorite table, where Darryl sat across from us, hanging his coat on the back of his chair. A few minutes later he had finished his burger and had moved on to the main course, a foot-high banana split with cherries on top.

"So," said Crank, "what's it like being an FBI agent?"

Darryl started coughing like a maniac. Arnie pounded him on the back.

"You know," said Arnie, "you should be more careful when you swallow."

Shaking off Arnie, Darryl glanced nervously at Crank and grunted, "What are you trying to do? You could blow my whole operation."

"Sorry," said Crank. "I was just curious."

Watching Darryl eat ice cream, I realized he was younger than I had thought. I figured he must be twenty-one, maybe twenty-two. Maybe he had just graduated from college. Still, he seemed older. When he smiled, there was something behind it that seemed cold and hard.

Arnie studied him. "Are you really in the FBI?"

Darryl wiped his mouth and checked the nearby tables, then lowered his voice. "I went to the FBI National Academy. Nine weeks of basic training with a coat and tie. When I graduated, I was sworn in by the chief himself."

"The chief?" I said.

He looked at me with contempt. "J. Edgar Hoover, director of the FBI. He shook my hand. This hand, right here."

Crank stared at Darryl's hand. "Wow," he said.

"I was assigned to Los Angeles," said Darryl. "I do background checks, surveillance, bag jobs."

"What's a bag job?" asked Crank.

"Searching a house or office. If there's anything important, you take a picture."

Oz said, "Isn't that illegal?"

"I'm keeping you safe," said Darryl.

Oz snorted. "From what, monster movies?"

Darryl flushed again. "This isn't my only case. I'm working on another one. A big one."

Crank's eyes lit up. "What is it?"

Oz said, "There isn't one. He's blowing smoke."

"Oh, yeah?" said Darryl. He glanced around to see if anyone was listening, then leaned forward. "There's a physics professor who may be leaking nuclear secrets to the Russians. He lives around here."

I thought of Klaus Fuchs, the Russian spy, and remembered what Mrs. Kramer had told us. Our enemies are all around. They're here. They're real.

Arnie gasped. "He's in Sierra Madre?"

Darryl shook his head, then looked down. I could tell that he'd said too much. Trying to change the subject, he said suddenly, "You want to see something cool?" He reached into his pocket and pulled out a rectangular metal object.

Arnie said, "Hey, a silver PEZ dispenser!"

"You idiot," said Crank. "That's not for candy."

Darryl set the object on the table. "It's a Minox. A state-of-the-art spy camera."

Crank gazed at it in awe. "Can I hold it?"

"Okay. Just be careful." Darryl handed the camera to Crank, who cradled it in his palm.

"It takes great pictures," said Darryl. "Especially closeups, for documents."

While the others checked out the camera, I kept glancing at the coat on the back of Darryl's chair, where he kept his notebook.

"Let me see the camera," I said. As I reached for it, I knocked over Darryl's drink, spilling it into his lap. Darryl jumped to his feet.

"Hey, watch it, will you?" he croaked.

"Sorry," I said.

He took a handful of napkins from the dispenser and tried wiping off his pants. Finally, embarrassed, he mumbled something and headed off to the bathroom.

As soon as he was gone, I reached into his coat pocket and pulled out the notebook.

Arnie's eyes grew big. "Geez, Paul, what are you doing?"

Crank grabbed my arm. "That's government property," he said, trying to wrestle away the notebook.

Oz took hold of Crank's arm and pulled. While they struggled, I thumbed quickly through the notebook, knowing I had just a minute or two to find what I was looking for. As I did, someone bellowed, "What's going on over here?"

My stomach dropped about three floors. I turned around, and there, wearing an apron, hands on his hips, stood D. His name was actually Dominic Bandini, and he owned the place.

"Hi, Mr. Bandini," I said, hiding the notebook under the table. "How's it going?"

"Not so good," he said. "Some people are fighting in my restaurant."

Arnie said, "You're not going to call my mom, are you?"

Just then I saw Darryl come out of the bathroom.

"We're fine, everything's fine," I said.

"It better be," said Mr. Bandini. "This is lunch, not a wrestling match."

The minute he turned away, I stuck the notebook back in Darryl's coat pocket. Darryl might have seen me if he hadn't been so busy trying to cover the wet spot on the front of his pants.

Darryl was pretty quiet after that. He put away his camera, then finished off the banana split. Tossing a few bills on the table, he rose and pulled on his coat. The notebook flopped out and fell to the floor. I held my breath.

He scooped it up and turned to us. "Gotta go. You guys have a way to get home?"

I nodded. "We can walk from here."

"See you around," he said, heading out the door.

When he was gone, Crank stared at me. "Are you crazy? He could have arrested us. We could have been charged with treason."

"Oh, please," said Oz.

"He's spying on Laura," I said. "After they argued, did you see the way he wrote in his notebook?"

"You're dreaming, all of you," said Crank.

"So, tell us," said Oz, eyeing me, "what was in the notebook?"

"Names," I said. "Don Siegel, Walter Wanger, Kevin McCarthy, Dana Wynter . . ."

"Laura Burke?" said Oz.

I shook my head. "Not as far as I saw. Then Mr. Bandini came over, and I had to put it back."

Crank said, "Who cares about that stuff? Did you hear what he said?"

"Who?" asked Arnie.

"Darryl! While you three were drooling over his notebook, he mentioned a real spy. The physics professor!"

"Hey, you're right," said Arnie. "Somebody's selling nuclear secrets right under our noses."

Crank said, "Now, there's a name I'd like to have."

"Maybe we've got it," I said.

"What do you mean?" asked Crank.

I looked nervously at Oz. I knew he wouldn't like what I was going to say. Crank, on the other hand, would love it. How could they be so different? How was it possible to be friends with two people who wanted to kill each other?

I took a deep breath. "When I was looking at the notebook, I saw something scribbled in the margin. It said *Richard Feynman, Cal Tech*."

8 · THE GENIUS

THE ALIENS WERE ATTACKING.

A fiery ray came shooting out of their ship, destroying everything in its path. Soldiers crouched behind a hill, loading their weapons.

Nearby, a priest watched. "I think we should try to make them understand we mean no harm," he said. "No real attempt has been made to communicate with them, you know."

The priest opened his Bible. Rising, he began moving toward the aliens.

"Though I walk through the valley of the shadow of death," he recited, "I will fear no evil. And I will dwell in the house of the Lord forever."

Zap!

Crank snorted. "So long, sucker."

Arnie crouched next to him, quivering.

"Great special effects," said Oz. "That's why they won an Academy Award."

We were at the Monster Matinee. Mr. Young, owner of the Sierra Madre Theater, showed horror movies every Saturday afternoon, and this week it was *The War of the Worlds*. Afterward, at D's, I sipped a root beer float and thought about the aliens.

"Why do they always want to kill people or take over the world?" I asked.

"Because they're aliens," said Crank.

"Why don't they read books or bake cookies or play baseball?"

"Bake cookies?" Crank shook his head. "Man, you're losing it."

Arnie said, "Paul's right. They travel through space, find intelligent life, and what do they do? Blow things up?"

"Why should they be any different from us?" said Oz.

Crank bit into an onion ring. "We don't blow things up," he said.

"Then why do we have drop drills?" I asked.

"It's not our fault," said Crank. "It's the Russians. We're just protecting ourselves."

"Oh, really?" said Oz. "How do you explain Hiroshima?"

Crank popped the onion ring into his mouth. "Self-defense. Read your history books."

"You really think so?" I said.

Arnie munched on a brownie, his eyes darting nervously around the table.

Crank's expression darkened. "Look, if you're so worried about getting blown up, why don't you do something about it?"

"Like what?" I asked.

"There's a Russian spy out there. We could find him."

No one spoke. In the kitchen, I could hear Mr. Bandini calling out orders. On the jukebox, Elvis Presley sang "That's All Right, Mama."

Crank said, "Remember what Mrs. Kramer told us? It's a war. We have to fight communism."

Arnie stared at him. "Us? Here?"

"Wake up," said Crank. "Things are happening. We could help."

Oz said, "This is nuts."

"The FBI doesn't think so," said Crank. "Look, we have the spy's name. He may be right down the street at Cal Tech. Let's see if we can find him. What's the harm in that?"

"What about the filming?" said Arnie. "I don't want to miss anything."

I said, "We can't go next week, remember? We have to wait until the week after, for spring break."

"See?" said Crank. "It's perfect. We can go see the guy after school."

I remembered the professor's name: Richard Feynman. I imagined him teaching a physics class, then ducking around the corner and transmitting a message to the Russians.

"I say we do it," I said.

Arnie swallowed hard. "Me too."

We looked at Oz. He sipped on his Coke, thinking.

"What's wrong?" Crank asked him, smiling thinly. "You chicken?"

Oz half-rose from his chair. I pushed him back down. "Stop it!" I told them, looking around for Mr. Bandini. "You want to get us thrown out?"

Oz glared at Crank. "I'll go with you. But not to help. I'm doing it to keep an eye on you."

"Oh, really?" said Crank.

Oz jabbed a finger at Crank's chest. "That's right, Mr. FBI. Don't try anything stupid. I'm watching you."

He gazed around the circle, his expression grim. Crank's smile faded. I tried to look brave. Arnie hugged his knees, shivering.

This wasn't a movie. It was real.

The California Institute of Technology, Cal Tech, was on a quiet street in Pasadena, less than a mile from Wilson Junior High. We walked there after school on Monday, lugging our books and wondering what we were getting into. It was a peaceful campus, with Spanish-style buildings and lots of trees. Students, most of them boys, strolled along well-kept paths, talking, smiling, joking.

"You know," said Arnie, looking around, "it's not that scary."

Oz said, "So, where's the spy?"

"Will you shut up?" said Crank. "He could be right here."

"Let's find out," I said. I approached one of the students, a thin young man with glasses who sat cross-legged on the grass with a pile of books next to him.

"Richard Feynman?" said the young man. "I think he's got a class this afternoon. He should be along in a minute."

We waited, and a short time later the student pointed across the lawn to a wiry dark-haired man who appeared to be in his thirties. The man wore wrinkled slacks and a white shirt with sleeves rolled up to the elbows. In one arm he carried a stack of books and in the other a bulging briefcase. Despite the weight, he moved along quickly, giving the impression of someone who was hurrying not because he wanted to get someplace but because that's just the way he was.

Crank watched for a minute, then started to follow him at a safe distance. I looked at Arnie and Oz. Oz shrugged, and we went along too. A few students glanced at us, probably wondering what thirteen-year-olds were doing on campus, but Feynman never noticed. He entered one of the buildings and disappeared inside a classroom. We positioned ourselves outside the door, which was open a crack, and looked through.

Feynman set down his things and went straight to the board while twenty students watched. He scribbled away, mumbling to himself, then turned back toward the class.

"Okay, look," he said, "I know you're not studying superfluidity, but I am. And I'm baffled."

He spoke the way he walked, in a hurry, almost stumbling

over his words. His accent reminded me of Mrs. Bonello, our next-door neighbor from Brooklyn. It made him sound more like a gangster than a college professor.

"For instance, liquid helium," he said. "Put it in a beaker, and what does it do? Just sit there, right? Wrong. It moves up and over the walls, as if there's no gravity. If there's a microscopic crack or hole in the glass that's too small for gas molecules, it glides right through. Or try this. Take two glass surfaces, polish them so they're perfectly smooth, then press them together as hard as you can. The liquid helium still passes between them. I don't understand."

"What if you freeze it?" asked a young woman in the front row.

"It won't freeze," said Feynman, "no matter how cold you make it."

"Maybe it's Kryptonite," said a young man behind her. He slumped down in his seat. "I'm starting to feel weak."

"I guess that explains your last test score," said Feynman. He turned to the rest of the class. "You know what the problem is? It's not the liquid helium. It's not our equipment. It's not the fact that Mr. Mulligan here is dying a slow, painful death, millions of miles from his home planet. The problem, ladies and gentlemen, is us. All of us. The only problem with liquid helium is that we haven't got enough imagination to figure it out."

After that, he launched into a lecture on quantum mechanics, a term I'd heard once or twice but had no clue about. He talked for nearly an hour, and I still had no clue.

When the lecture ended, the students clustered around Feynman, firing off questions. He answered most of them but seemed preoccupied. Then, glancing at his watch, he grabbed his books and briefcase and exploded out the door. Arnie started to follow, but Crank grabbed his sleeve.

"Wait a second," said Crank.

Most of the students were gathering up their things, but the one called Mulligan was back at his desk, writing furiously in a notebook. When the others left, Crank entered the room, and we went along.

"You're pretty quick with that pen," said Crank.

Mulligan looked up. "Huh?"

Crank said, "You know, faster than a speeding bullet."

Mulligan chuckled. "Oh, that. Yeah, I wish I really was Superman. I could use his brain. You need it to keep up with Feynman."

Crank glanced at us. "Me and my friends, we were outside, listening."

"Did you follow what he was saying?" asked Mulligan. "If you did, I wish you'd explain it to me."

I said, "If you didn't understand, what were you writing?"

"Questions," he said. "That's Feynman's big thing. He says you can figure out just about anything if you ask the right questions. Of course, it helps to be a genius."

Arnie gaped at him. "Are you a genius?"

Mulligan laughed. "Not me, Feynman. Some people say he's the greatest physicist since Albert Einstein. He has more brainpower in his toenail clippings than I have in my whole body."

"Yuck," said Arnie.

"Does he ever mention the bomb?" asked Crank.

Oz shot him a look, but Crank didn't see it. His attention was riveted on Mulligan, looking for an answer, listening for clues.

"No, he doesn't," said Mulligan.

I could see Crank sag a little, disappointed.

"Which is odd," Mulligan went on, "because he was in on it from the beginning."

"What do you mean?" asked Crank.

"Didn't you know?" said Mulligan. "He was one of the leaders of the Manhattan Project. He helped develop the atomic bomb. And for some reason he doesn't like to talk about it."

9 · NUCLEAR SECRETS

"It's him. I know it," said Crank.

"You don't know anything," said Oz.

Crank stuck out his chin, the way he did when he was being stubborn. "He's leaking information to the Russians about the bomb. He helped invent it."

Arnie said, "Can we stop arguing? My stomach hurts."

It was Tuesday, the day after our trip to Cal Tech, and we had gone to Oz's house after school. There was no sign of Mr. Feldman. The door to his room was shut. But Bernice was there.

"Come on, eat, eat!" she said, emerging from the kitchen with a plate of chopped liver and matzo. When she wasn't driving the liberalmobile, she was in the kitchen preparing food. She was alarmed by Arnie's scrawny chest, and she knew in her heart of hearts that Oz would be tall if only she could feed him enough chicken soup and stuffed cabbage.

Oz spread chopped liver on a piece of matzo and passed the plate to the rest of us. Arnie sampled it.

"Hey," he said, "how come my mother's liver doesn't taste like this?"

Bernice shook her head sadly. "You mother doesn't cook liver. She punishes it."

I tried some of the chopped liver, but Crank was too wound up to eat. He waited until Bernice had left the room, then lowered his voice and said, "We need to investigate."

"Who?" said Oz. "Arnie's mother?"

"That's right, Feldman, laugh it off," said Crank. "Meanwhile, the cold war is being fought on your doorstep."

Oz glanced toward his father's room. "Not on the doorstep," he said. "In my house."

Arnie said, "That professor seemed nice enough to me."

Crank stared at him. "Feynman? He could be on the phone to Moscow right now." Crank reached into a stack of books next to him. "I've been reading up on that other spy, Klaus Fuchs. He passed information to the Russians, and a few years later, they had the bomb. He confessed it all. He's in prison now." Crank turned to Oz. "Not so funny, huh?"

I added, "Mulligan said that Feynman likes questions—but not about the bomb. Don't you think that's strange?"

"You guys are crazy," said Oz.

Crank said, "You think he's going to have horns and green skin? He's a spy. He's supposed to blend in."

"It's like the body snatchers," I said. "You can't tell who they are. It could be anyone."

"Stop it, would you?" said Arnie. "You're creeping me out."

"Look," said Oz, "I think Feynman's innocent. But even if he's not, shouldn't the FBI handle it?"

"Darryl's tied up with the movie," said Crank. "It might be weeks before he can check out Feynman. We can help."

"What do you think we should do?" I asked.

Arnie said, "Just so you know, I hate guns."

"We could hang around, check him out, watch what he does," said Crank. "It wouldn't be hard."

"What if I'm right and he's innocent?" said Oz.

"Then that's the end of it," said Crank. "Feynman will be off the hook, and Darryl won't need to investigate."

"And if you're right?" I asked Crank.

He didn't say anything. He just looked at me. I tried to guess what he was thinking, but with Crank you could never be sure.

"Where's the phone book?" he asked.

Oz pulled one out of a drawer and handed it to him. Thumbing through it, Crank grinned. "Here's a listing for Richard Feynman. He lives in Altadena."

Altadena was the town next to Sierra Madre, at the base of the San Gabriel Mountains. Sometimes we rode there on our bikes to go hiking.

Crank copied the address and phone number on a piece of paper, then closed the phone book.

"We start tomorrow," he said.

The next day at school, Mrs. Kramer told us about the Korean War and how the Communists had brainwashed American soldiers. I tried to listen, but all I could think about was Richard Feynman. Would we see him? What would he do? Was he spying for the Russians, the way Klaus Fuchs had been?

After school we hopped on our bikes and rode over to Altadena. No one said much. Crank was grim. Oz looked doubtful. Arnie kept sucking on Pepto-Bismol tablets.

Feynman lived on Alameda Street, just west of Lake Avenue. We parked our bikes around the corner so no one would get suspicious, then walked down Alameda toward his house.

Crank glanced at Arnie. "You look nervous. Act natural."

"How do I do that?" asked Arnie.

Oz said, "Try picking your nose."

Crank pulled out a slip of paper and checked the address. "Okay, guys, there it is," he said, nodding toward a place across the street.

It didn't look like the home of a genius. It was half of a duplex, two small houses crowded into one lot with a shared wall and driveway. Feynman's house was painted dark red, with green shutters and a row of bushes in front. In the yard, a woman was watering the flowers.

Arnie ducked behind Crank. "She might see us!"

"You idiot!" said Crank. "Hiding is the worst thing you can do."

I said, "That must be his wife."

"How do you know?" asked Crank.

"I just assumed."

"Don't assume anything," he said. "It's the first rule of investigation."

I looked at Oz. He rolled his eyes.

The woman finished and went inside. A short time later, Feynman came out. Next to him was a strange dark-haired man with a wild look in his eye. The two of them were deep in conversation.

Crank and I exchanged looks. I wondered if he was thinking the same thing I was. He nodded and mouthed the word: "Russian."

Whoever the man was, you didn't see people like him every day, at least not in Sierra Madre. He had a broad nose, a bushy black beard, fiery eyes, and a funny little cap. He wore work boots, and his shirt and pants were stained. As we watched, he and Feynman came right toward us.

"Don't panic," Crank whispered, "Just pretend we're having a regular conversation."

"What should we say?" asked Arnie.

"Anything," said Crank.

Arnie said, "I pledge allegiance to the flag—"

"Cut it out!" said Crank.

"Uh, guys," I said, "they're getting away."

They had veered off down the sidewalk, heading toward Lake Avenue. Feynman was moving fast, like that day on campus. It was hard to keep up. As it turned out, they wouldn't have noticed us anyway. They were gesturing and talking excitedly.

As the two of them approached the corner, they moved toward a small foreign car that was parked at the curb. The other man reached into his pocket and pulled out a set of keys.

Crank whispered, "They're making a break for it!"

"What'll we do?" Arnie whined.

"Follow them!" said Crank. He took off toward the bikes, which were parked just around the corner. Arnie stumbled after him.

The car started up, eased away from the curb, and chugged off down the street. Crank and Arnie climbed onto their bikes. Oz just stood there, watching.

"Come on!" I said. "We don't want to lose them."

Oz sighed. "You too?"

I said, "Think of it this way. Remember all those chase scenes in the movies? This is our chance to be in one."

I took off after Crank. Oz hesitated for a moment, then followed.

The car stopped at the corner, then turned right onto Lake. Crank and Arnie jumped their bikes off the curb and took off after it. I got my bike and hurried to catch up, with Oz right behind, both of us pedaling as fast as we could. We turned onto Lake and accelerated, helped by the downhill slope.

Suddenly brake lights flashed, and the car jerked to a stop at a traffic signal. When it did, Crank almost crashed into the rear bumper. Arnie, pedaling like a lunatic, nearly ran into Crank. Oz and I skidded to a stop beside them, our rear wheels fishtailing.

I checked to see if Feynman and his friend had spotted us, but they showed no sign of it. Inside the car they continued to talk and gesture.

The light turned green, and they hung a right onto New York Drive, a few blocks south of Alameda. The car picked up speed. So did we. By that time we were flying across the pavement, dodging cars and pedestrians.

As Crank and Arnie sped past, a woman stepped off the curb carrying a bag of groceries. Oz and I swerved and managed to avoid her. Behind us, a horn blared. A man yelled, "Hey you kids, watch it!"

Shaken but determined, we took off again. Up ahead, the car turned right onto El Molino. We turned a few moments later. With a burst of speed I pulled up alongside Crank.

"They're going in circles," I said.

Crank, pedaling furiously, was wheezing like an accordion. "It's a trick. They're trying to shake us."

"They don't even know we're here," I said.

"Don't be so sure."

In the movies, the good guys catch the bad guys. In real life, sometimes it's all you can do to keep up, especially if you're riding a bike.

Ahead of us, at the top of a hill, the car turned right onto Calaveras. When we got there, it turned right again on

Lake, where there were some little stores and businesses. We pedaled to the corner and pulled our bikes onto the sidewalk, panting like dogs.

Crank shook his head. "We lost them."

"Now what?" I asked.

"My stomach feels weird," said Arnie. He popped another handful of Pepto-Bismol tablets. There were little pink flecks around his mouth.

"You better not get sick," said Crank.

Oz said, "Yeah, it's the second rule of investigation. Don't throw up."

Just then, a familiar shape caught my eye. "The car!"

It was parked at the curb on Lake Avenue, a block down the street in front of a dry cleaners. But there was no sign of Feynman or the strange man.

Crank surveyed the area. "Okay, guys, this is it. Leave your bikes here and fan out."

"No way," said Oz. "This is stupid. I'm not fanning."

Crank stepped toward Oz, glaring at him.

Moving between them, I said, "What if we split up? Oz and I can take the right side of the street. Crank, you and Arnie take the left. We'll find them."

We didn't. Ten minutes later, we huddled near the car.

"I'm starved," said Arnie. "I want to go home."

Crank glared at him. "You think FBI agents go home when they're hungry? Suck it up, pal."

Another twenty minutes passed. I know it was twenty

minutes because Arnie announced the time every thirty seconds or when his stomach growled, whichever came first.

I was ready to call it quits when we spotted Feynman and his friend coming out of a restaurant called the Kopper Kettle. They walked toward us, and we ducked out of sight. Reaching the car, they climbed in.

"The bikes!" said Crank. "What were we thinking?"

Our bikes were parked a block away. As we watched, helpless, the car pulled away and disappeared around the corner.

"Can we go home now?" said Arnie.

I looked at Crank. "You really think Feynman's a spy?"

"Did you see his buddy?" said Crank. "This proves it."

Oz said, "Don't assume anything. Remember? We saw him with a friend, that's all."

Crank said, "You know what I saw? An American scientist giving away nuclear secrets. We have to find out more."

"We could tap his phone," said Oz.

Crank considered it, then shook his head. "Not enough time."

Oz stared at him. "I was joking."

"There's something else we could do," said Crank. "Of course, it would be risky."

Arnie blinked real fast. "You think it might be dangerous?"

"Maybe," said Crank, gazing off into the distance.

"What is it?" I asked.

"We need to meet the enemy in his lair."

"What's that supposed to mean?" said Oz.

"Gentlemen," said Crank, "I think it's time to have a little chat with Professor Feynman."

10 · GUILTY!

FREEDOM!

It was Friday, and school was out for spring break. For us, the next week would be busy. We were going to Hollywood to see more filming. If we were lucky, we'd be spending time with Laura. And there was the small matter of a Russian spy.

Crank was determined to speak with Feynman. Arnie, of course, was scared. This time, Oz and I were too. We tried to talk Crank out of it, but he wouldn't listen.

We approached Feynman after class that afternoon as he was putting his lecture notes back into his briefcase.

"Professor Feynman," said Crank, "can we talk to you for a minute?"

"You're doing it," he said without looking up.

Crank said, "My friends and I are, uh, writing a paper for school. It's about the Manhattan Project."

With those words, Feynman's head jerked up. He stared intently at Crank. There was something in his gaze—anger or maybe fear. Then he turned back to the briefcase and latched it.

"Sorry, boys. I have work to do."

"Really?" said Crank suspiciously. "Like what?"

Feynman managed a weak smile. "If you really have to know, I'm going to my office to grade papers."

"Can we walk you there?" asked Crank.

Arnie added, "I could carry your briefcase."

"You think so?" said Feynman.

Arnie grabbed the handle and slid the briefcase off the desk. It dropped to the floor with a thud. He looked up in amazement. "What's in there?"

Feynman said, "A bowling ball. An anvil. Nothing much."

"I'll get it," said Crank. He lifted the briefcase with ease.

Feynman eyed him, then shrugged. "You want to come along, fine. But I've only got a few minutes."

He hurried out the door and across campus. As we struggled to keep up, I thought of all the times I had huddled under my desk at school, waiting for the bomb. The man walking with us had helped to invent it. He had seen the first explosion.

"What was it like?" I said. "You know, that test in the desert. I heard that the mushroom cloud was ten miles high. I heard it vaporized the cactus."

It was a warm day, but I could swear that he shivered. "You want to do a paper for school? Write it about science."

"What do you mean?" I asked.

"You like mysteries?"

I shrugged. "Sure."

We passed under a tree, and he pointed to a branch. "See that bird? Maybe it's a robin or a finch. For some people, that's all they want to know. They think if you name it, you understand it. But when I look at that bird, all I can think about is one question. How does it fly?"

Arnie stopped and gazed at the bird. "How *does* it fly?"

Feynman kept moving. Arnie ran to catch up.

"Well," said Feynman, "I could spout all kinds of formulas to explain it, but the truth is, we're not really sure how birds fly. It's a mystery."

He strode across a grassy lawn, still gesturing. "Lots of things are mysteries. People think they know the answers when they know the names. Meanwhile, there's one guy standing off in a corner asking, 'But why? How? What's going on here?' That's a scientist. Solving mysteries. Looking for the truth."

I said, "It sounds hard."

"Of course it's hard," he said. "Look, you've got two choices in life. You can take the easy way—float along, believe what they tell you. Or you can take the hard way—ask questions, think about the answers, demand the truth. It's tough. Sometimes it hurts. But it's your job. You're human. That's what it's all about, right?"

He ducked into a building and led us down a quiet

hallway, stopping in front of a door that had his name on it. He tried the handle and shook his head in disgust. "Locked out again."

"Don't you have a key?" asked Oz.

"Hate 'em," said Feynman. "I keep my doors unlocked. Only problem is, sometimes the custodians forget."

Pulling a paper clip from his pocket, he knelt and inserted it into the keyhole. He jiggled it around, head cocked as if listening for something. A moment later there was a click, and the door swung open.

"How did you do that?" asked Oz.

Climbing to his feet, Feynman pocketed the clip and smiled. "It's not hard. I learned years ago."

Crank said, "At Los Alamos? On the Manhattan Project?"

Feynman studied him. "As a matter of fact, yes." He turned to Oz. "It was a challenge, you know? A game. Once or twice I opened the master safe. Couldn't believe how easy it was."

I looked at Crank. His lips were set in a grim line.

Feynman entered his office and invited us in. The place looked as if it had been hit by a tornado. The desk was littered with books and soft-drink bottles. In the middle was a stack of papers weighed down by a beat-up stapler.

Feynman gestured toward the stack. "Captain Ahab had the whale. I've got papers to grade. They're after me, boys. I can't get away."

On the wall hung a photograph showing a group of about

thirty people in a desert setting. Crank set the briefcase on a chair and approached the photo to inspect it.

"Was this at Los Alamos?" he asked.

Feynman went to his desk and made a show of searching for something. "Huh? Oh, that? Yeah, I suppose so."

"It must have been exciting," said Arnie. "I mean, you saved the country, right? We won the war."

"Some people would say that," replied Feynman.

I noticed a second photo on the wall. It showed Feynman standing beside a man with neatly trimmed hair, a coat and tie, and round-rimmed glasses. There was something familiar about him.

"Was this at Los Alamos too?" I asked.

Feynman nodded.

"Who's that with you?" I asked.

"A friend of mine. One of the other scientists."

"What was his name?" asked Crank.

"Klaus Fuchs," said Feynman.

"Guilty!" said Crank.

"You're nuts," said Oz.

"Hey, where's Arnie?" I asked.

Our meeting with Richard Feynman was over, and we were getting on the bus to go home. Crank had hoped for a longer visit so we could look around the office for more clues, but after talking about the photos, Feynman had asked us to leave so he could grade papers.

"There he is," said Oz, pointing.

Arnie was in front of a drugstore by the bus stop, sitting on a coin-operated pig, reading a comic book, and munching on a candy bar.

"I'll get him," said Crank darkly. While the driver held the bus, Crank stepped off and returned a moment later, gripping Arnie's arm like a vise.

"Hey, I was busy!" Arnie whined.

"You'll be real busy in a minute," said Crank. "I'm going to dangle you out the window by your feet."

I told the driver, "He's just kidding. They're actually close friends."

"After that," said Crank, "I'll set your eyebrows on fire."

We took seats near the back. I noticed that the driver kept glancing at us in the rearview mirror.

Oz said, "I'm telling you, Feynman's not a spy."

"Oh, yeah?" said Crank. "Then why was he friends with Klaus Fuchs?"

"It was just a picture," said Oz.

"Where does Superman leave his clothes?" asked Arnie.

"Huh?" I said.

"Okay, so Clark Kent goes into a phone booth. He changes into Superman, right? What happens to his clothes?"

"Your mind," I said, "is an amazing thing."

"He doesn't just leave them, does he?" asked Arnie. "I mean, think about it. He'd have dirty laundry all over town. Pants, suits, shirts. Underwear, for God's sake."

Crank turned back to Oz. "It wasn't just the photo. Feynman didn't want to talk about it. He was hiding something."

"You're dreaming," said Oz.

Crank said, "He picks locks! When he was at Los Alamos, he broke into the master safe. Can you imagine what they kept there? I'm sure the Russians wanted to know."

Oz shook his head. "You just proved my point. If he was stealing secrets, you think he'd tell us about the safe?"

"Of course he would!" said Crank. "We're a bunch of kids. That's the beauty of this whole operation."

Operation? Is that what this was? *Operation Feynman.* I liked the sound of it.

"So, what are you saying?" asked Arnie.

Crank glared at him. "What do you think, dipwad? He's a spy."

"Superman?" said Arnie. "No way!"

Crank slugged him.

Arnie yelped, "Hey, what was that for?"

"You're an idiot," said Crank.

The phone rang.

"I'll get it," I called.

It was later that night, after dinner. My mom and dad were watching TV in the living room. I was in the den, reading about Los Alamos in the encyclopedia.

As I reached for the phone, my dad burst into the room, a tense expression on his face. "Don't touch that! It's for me."

"How do you know?" I asked.

He picked up the receiver. Instead of hello, he said, "Gerald Smith." It sounded strange, as if he was at work. He listened for a moment, then cradled the phone against his chest.

"How about some privacy, huh?" He seemed mad at me.

I took the encyclopedia into the hallway, and he closed the door behind me. I don't know why, but I wanted to hear what he was saying. Maybe I was mad too. Maybe I was tired of being the only kid in my school who wasn't sure what his father did.

I looked around to see if anyone was watching, then put my ear against the door. He was talking in low tones, so I couldn't make out much of what he was saying, but I caught a few words.

Payload. Radar. Bomber.

"What are you doing?"

I whirled around and saw Lulu standing in the hallway door, minding my business.

"Get out of here!" I whispered, but it was too late.

She turned and ran into the living room. "Mom," she called, "Paul's spying on Daddy!"

Just then, the door to the den opened. My father stood there, glaring down at me. He grabbed me by the arm and marched me into the living room, where my mother sat wide-eyed, holding my sister.

"Lulu," she said in a pinched voice, "go to your room, please."

Lulu looked at my father, then at me. "You're in big trouble now," she said, and pranced out of the room.

"What did you hear?" asked my father.

There was something big and dark in our house. I was tired of tiptoeing around it. I wanted to kick it, puncture it, see what came out.

"You make bombers," I said.

He glared at my mother. She dropped her gaze, as if what I had done was her fault. Then she looked back up at him. "You told me. Maybe you should tell Paul."

"He's not supposed to know. It's classified."

"He's your son," she said.

Was I? I felt like some kind of interplanetary exchange student—a Martian, maybe, sent to find out what junior high school was like on earth. Or maybe my parents were the aliens, uncomfortable in their bodies, stationed far from home.

My mother blurted, "Your father designs planes to carry the atomic bomb."

"Shut up!" he said in a strangled voice. "Shut up!"

I stared at my father. I'd never heard that much feeling in his voice.

"Not another word," he told her. "I'm warning you."

She said, "It's all right, dear. Your secret is safe with us."

PART TWO
YOU'RE NEXT!

11 · IT'S ALIVE!

THERE WAS A POD ON THE POOL TABLE.

Miles and Becky had been called to their friend Jack's house. Jack and his wife, Teddy, met them at the door. When they went inside, Jack took the cover off the pool table and showed them a body that had mysteriously appeared. It looked like Jack, except the face was smooth and unlined, as if all worries had been erased. Miles got an ink pad and took its fingerprints. They were blank, like the face.

Jack poured himself a drink. His hand was shaking so badly that he dropped the glass and cut himself. Later that night, after Miles and Becky had left, Jack nodded off. As soon as he did, the body's eyes flew open. Teddy noticed and went to look. There was a cut on the hand, exactly where Jack's had been. It was bleeding.

She screamed, "It's alive! It's alive!"

We were in Hollywood. It was the first day of spring break, and the film crew was shooting a scene in a little house on

Rodney Drive. When it was over, I found that my hands were shaking as badly as Jack's.

I turned to my friends. "Did that bother anybody else?"

Arnie licked his lips. His eyes were as big as coasters. "Fine!" he said. "I'm fine."

"It's just a movie," growled Crank, but I noticed that his face was kind of chalky.

Oz said, "Did you notice the lighting? Ellsworth Fredericks is a genius."

"Who's he?" I asked.

He stared at me. "The cinematographer. Pay attention, huh?"

We found Laura outside. She waved to us and came over. "You made it!" she said. "I didn't know if you'd be here."

"We had to come," I said. "I've got your magazines."

I gave them back, thanking Laura and telling her how much I had enjoyed the story. As we spoke, I studied her face. I'd been dreaming of her for a week and had wondered if I'd be disappointed when I saw her again. I shouldn't have worried. She was more beautiful than ever.

"How did it go last week?" I asked her.

"Nothing very exciting. We were in the Valley, shooting exteriors. A train station, a country club, a house. You didn't miss much."

Oz checked his watch. "We should probably be going. Our bus comes in a few minutes."

"Forget the bus," she said. "I can drive you home."

I said, "You don't have to do that."

"To be honest, I'd like the company," she said. "That scene scared me. Besides, I could use some help. I have some things I'd like to drop off at my house."

"Thanks," I told her. "That would be great."

We helped Laura carry her things to the car, a blue Plymouth sedan. When she unlocked the trunk and opened it, she dropped what she was holding and screamed.

I hurried over beside her. She turned away from the car and threw her arms around me, shaking. Looking over her shoulder, I peered into the trunk.

There was a pod inside.

Out from behind a tree jumped Darryl. "Surprise!" Stepping over to the trunk, he looked down at the pod and grinned. "Great, huh? I borrowed it from the prop department."

I said, "Are you crazy? You scared her to death."

"Lighten up," said Darryl. "And while you're at it, get your hands off my girl."

Laura moved away from me and faced him. "You're awful."

Darryl said, "Well, aren't you going to open it?"

"Open what?" asked Laura.

"The pod."

Laura shivered. "You're not just awful. You're sick."

"Oh, come on," said Darryl. He lifted the top off the pod. Inside was a bouquet of flowers, which he picked up and offered to her. "I was trying to be nice. I wanted to say I'm sorry."

"You've got a strange way of showing it," said Laura.

The last time I'd seen them together, outside the nursery in Sierra Madre, they had been arguing. Thinking of Darryl's notebook, I wondered why he wanted to apologize. Was he really interested in Laura, or did he have other motives?

"I'll buy you a drink," he told her. "We can kiss and make up."

I glared at him. At that moment, I couldn't imagine hating anyone more.

Next to me, Laura was thinking. Finally she shook her head. "Keep your flowers. And while you're at it, take the pod, too."

"What about the drink?" he asked.

Laura said, "I'm busy. I'm taking my friends home."

He studied her for a moment. His gaze grew hard and cold. He reached into the trunk, took the pod, and walked off.

Watching him, Laura said, "Let's go, boys."

We loaded the rest of her things into the trunk and got in the car. Laura fumbled for her keys. I noticed that her hand was still shaking. Starting the car, she drove us up Rodney Drive to Ambrose Avenue, where she turned right and pulled up in front of a neatly painted green bungalow.

"Is that your house?" I asked.

She nodded. "I bought it a couple of years ago."

We unloaded her things from the trunk and helped her carry them to the house. Inside, the rooms were neat and tidy. After we finished, she took us into the kitchen and poured us all a glass of lemonade.

Sipping my drink, I looked over at Oz and saw that he was wondering the same thing I was. How could a part-time actress afford to buy a house?

A half hour later, she dropped us off in downtown Sierra Madre.

"Thanks for the lift," I said. "See you tomorrow?"

She said, "I don't think so. Don Siegel called a production meeting. I'm not even sure they'll be filming."

She must have seen the disappointment in our faces, because she quickly added, "You can come on Wednesday, though. We'll be on the soundstage."

"What's that?" asked Arnie.

"A stage for filming indoors," said Oz. "It's at the studio."

Arnie said, "We're going to a Hollywood studio?"

Laura nodded. "Allied Artists. The address is on the shooting schedule."

"Will they let us in?" I asked.

She said, "I'll make sure they do. Let's meet at the front gate, around nine o'clock."

"Thanks," I said. "We'll be there."

She smiled, then waved and drove off, her hair blowing in the breeze.

The Russian was on the move.

With no filming the next day, we had biked over to Altadena, not sure of what to do but drawn there out of curiosity about Feynman. Riding past his house, we saw no signs of activity. We parked our bikes and walked up Lake Avenue. Arnie pulled out his PEZ dispenser and found there was nothing to dispense, so we headed for a little market.

That was when we saw him.

He was driving up Lake Avenue in the same foreign car we had seen the previous week. When he parked the car and got out, he appeared to be wearing the same shirt, pants, and odd little cap as before.

Crank muttered, "Don't those people ever change clothes?"

"What people?" I asked.

"Russians."

The man took a canvas satchel from the car, slung it over one shoulder, and set out on foot. We followed at a safe distance. I wondered what was in the satchel.

When the man reached a self-service laundry, he paused for a minute, then ducked inside.

"Maybe it's a rendezvous," said Crank.

"A what?" asked Arnie.

Crank said, "A secret meeting. Come on, let's get closer."

The four of us edged up to the laundry and peered through

the front window. The man was inside, studying a bulletin board that was covered with notes.

"He must be checking for messages," said Crank. "Clever."

As we watched, the man turned in our direction, and we ducked. Then he charged out the door, and we took off after him again. Every once in a while he paused and turned. Crank would whisper, "Scatter!" We would spread out and pretend to be window-shopping.

Once Arnie said, "I'm not shopping here. This is a beauty parlor."

Crank grabbed the back of Arnie's neck and squeezed.

"Ow!" said Arnie.

"You'll never make it in the FBI," said Crank.

The man strode up Lake Avenue to the corner, where he crossed the street to a barber shop. As he approached, Richard Feynman walked out.

"Bingo!" said Crank.

Feynman said something, and they headed down the street.

"What should we do?" asked Arnie.

"Keep following!" said Crank. "Don't lose them."

We trailed the two men, being careful not to look suspicious. Whenever they stopped, we stopped. We pretended to talk. We did more window-shopping.

At one store Arnie whispered, "Can I go in? They have the new Flash Gordon lunch pail."

"You wouldn't be able to use it," said Crank, gripping his arm. "You'd be dead."

Arnie said, "I'm not really that interested."

"Look, they're going to that restaurant again!" I said. "The Kopper Kettle."

The men went inside. We approached the place cautiously.

Arnie said, "Now what do we do?"

"Look inconspicuous," said Crank.

A moment later the door opened, and the Russian stuck his head out. "You guys want to join us?"

We stared at him.

He said, "You've been staying so far back. Don't you want to come closer? You could sit right next to us."

Crank said, "We didn't—I mean—"

"Sure, we'd love to," said Oz. "Right, guys?"

The man held open the door. Oz smiled and went inside.

"I don't know about this," muttered Crank.

I glanced at Arnie. He shrugged, and we moved toward the door. Crank hesitated, then followed.

The name Kopper Kettle made the place sound quaint and colorful, but it was really just a coffee shop. Inside, the man led us to a corner booth, where Feynman sat. On the table in front of him were two cups of coffee. The satchel was on the seat next to him.

The man said, "These are the kids who were following us."

Feynman looked up warily and studied us. "Don't I know you?"

I tried to keep my voice from shaking. "We were writing a paper for school, remember?"

"Oh, yeah," said Arnie.

"I said they could sit with us," the man told Feynman.

Feynman shrugged. "Fine."

The man said, "I'm Jirayr Zorthian. My friends call me Jerry."

Jerry? That didn't sound like a Russian spy. His accent didn't sound Russian either. Up close, the wild look in his eye was more of a twinkle. And I was struck by how small he was—nearly as short as Oz.

"Have a seat, kids," said Zorthian, sliding into the booth. As we did, a red-haired waitress approached, wearing a checkered apron and carrying an order pad.

"This is Hazel," said Zorthian. "Hazel, these are some friends of ours."

She eyed us skeptically. "Are you boys going to eat anything, or do you plan to freeload like these two?"

"Hey," said Zorthian, "we leave good tips."

"Yeah," she said, "I remember the last one. You wrote it on the back of your check. 'Get a new job.'"

"You should," said Zorthian. "You're too good for this place."

"Tell that to my boss," she said.

We ordered Cokes, and Hazel went to get them. When we

had spoken to Feynman before, he had encouraged us to ask questions. I decided to give it a try.

"So," I said, working up my courage, "what are you guys doing?"

Zorthian looked over at Feynman. "What do you think, Dick? Should we tell them?"

"Go ahead," said Feynman.

"Well," Zorthian told us, "you might say we've negotiated a trade."

Crank's eyes widened. I could imagine what he was thinking. Were they trading information? technology? nuclear secrets?

Zorthian said, "I never had much science in school, so Dick teaches me about physics. In exchange, he meets me here."

"He buys you food?" said Arnie.

Zorthian laughed. "No, it's not food."

"Then what is it?" asked Crank.

Zorthian looked at Feynman. Feynman nodded. Opening his satchel, Zorthian took out a handful of pencils and some paper.

"We draw," he said.

12 · PITCHFORKS AND HUBCAPS

ZORTHIAN SPREAD THE SHEETS OF PAPER ON THE TABLE. They were covered with sketches of a woman—standing straight, bending over, rubbing her back, carrying things. Some of the sketches were so full of life they seemed to jump off the page. Others just sat there.

Oz picked up one of the sketches and studied it. "Hey, isn't this Hazel?"

Zorthian chuckled. "You must be getting better, Dick. That's one of yours." He turned to us and said, "You should have seen the first ones he did. One looked like a monkey. The other was more like a moose."

"Hey," said Feynman.

"If you can draw people, you can draw anything," Zorthian said. "Hazel is a wonderful subject. She's the reason we come here."

I heard someone behind us and saw Hazel with a tray of drinks, looking over Oz's shoulder at Feynman's sketch.

"The nose is too big," she said.

Feynman shrugged. "I just draw what I see."

Hazel set the drinks in front of us. She said, "He's a famous scientist, you know. I'd hit him, but I'm afraid he'd get mad and blow up the place."

Feynman studied her as she went off to work the other tables. Grabbing a pencil, he started to sketch. Zorthian watched, making suggestions. Handing out pencils and paper, he invited us to try. My drawing didn't look much like Hazel. Neither did Arnie's, which made sense when he explained that it was a flying saucer.

Feynman was working with an intensity I recognized from watching him in class. Using his eyes and pencil, he was asking questions and looking for answers.

"It seems strange for a scientist to like drawing," I said.

"It shouldn't," said Zorthian. "People like Dick and me, we have a lot in common. We study the world to see the way it really is. We use our imaginations. We search for the truth and try to put it on paper. Then we look at what we've done and try again. If we're good, maybe each time we get a little closer."

He gestured across the room. "Take Hazel over there. She's one person out of billions. But if I can draw her just right, maybe I'll understand them all."

I said, "What if you look at the world and don't like what you see?" I glanced down at Arnie's drawing. "Maybe there really are flying saucers. Maybe there are monsters."

"Sometimes I think there are," said Zorthian. "But I'll tell you this. The most frightening thing isn't what you know. It's what you don't know. It's a scary world. You try to learn about it so you're not scared. Don't run away from the monsters. Move closer. Study them. Draw them. Try to figure them out."

"I can't," I said.

Feynman looked up from his drawing. He gazed at me for a long time. Finally he said, "Neither can I."

With sudden feeling, he snatched his sketch from the table, wadded it up, and threw it aside.

"Let's get out of here," he said. He dropped some money on the table and got up.

"My house?" asked Zorthian.

Feynman nodded. Zorthian watched him, then turned to us and said, "Want to come?"

It wasn't a house. It was a world, on forty-five acres at the top of Fair Oaks Avenue in the foothills of Altadena.

We stood next to the car and looked out over Zorthian's land as he described it. Using discarded materials, he had built everything he needed to sustain himself. There was a smokehouse, bakery, slaughterhouse, blacksmith shop, tannery, cobbler's bench, and ceramic kiln. The barn was made of railroad ties. Next to it was a sculptured wall of boulders and concrete chunks decorated with beer bottles, pitchforks, and hubcaps. The house itself was built out of old redwood timbers and colored glass insulators. Goats, sheep, and chickens roamed the property. In the distance, Pasadena was spread out before us. Beyond that, glistening in the sun, was Hollywood.

Feynman seemed to have perked up. "Jerry's one of the most famous muralists in the world," he said, "but some of us think this place is his greatest creation."

Zorthian said, "I call it the Center for Research and Development of Industrial Discards."

"Even his car is a discard," said Feynman. "He found it at a junkyard."

"That doesn't stop you from borrowing it," Zorthian said.

Feynman snorted. "I have to. My wife uses ours to haul her jewelry."

Arnie looked out over the land. "This place sure is big. Does anyone else live here?"

Zorthian smiled sadly. "I used to have a wife, but she left. She claimed I loved this place more than her."

He gave us a tour, then took us inside. We sat at a redwood table, where he poured a glass of milk for each of us. I tried mine and made a face. Zorthian smiled.

"It's goat's milk," he said. "I have all the food I need up here— milk and cheese from the goats, fresh eggs from the chickens, vegetables from the garden. Just like when I was a kid."

"Jerry's Armenian," said Feynman. "He was born in Turkey."

"Where's that?" asked Arnie.

"Near Greece," said Zorthian. "Right next to Russia."

Crank stared. It didn't take a mind reader to see what he was thinking.

"I like to do things with my hands," said Zorthian. "But Dick, he uses his mind. He was on the Manhattan Project, you know. The smartest people in the world, all crammed together in one place. Can you imagine what that was like?"

Feynman fidgeted, as if the room was getting warm.

Zorthian elbowed him playfully. "Some things never change, though. Even then, he mooched off his friends. Every weekend, he borrowed a car from Klaus Fuchs."

Arnie shot me a look. Even Oz seemed surprised. I watched Crank. He nodded grimly. "Funny how that name keeps popping up. What was he like, anyway?"

"Who?" asked Feynman.

"Klaus Fuchs," said Crank. "You know, the spy."

Feynman studied his hands for a moment, then looked up defiantly. "He was my friend."

"He was a traitor," said Crank.

Feynman rose abruptly from the table. For a minute I thought he was going to leave. Then he turned around to face us. There was a haunted look in his eyes.

"Do you ever want to get away?" he asked.

I thought of my father and mother and the dark thing that lived in our house.

"I do," I said.

"So do I," said Feynman. "That's why I come here with

Jerry. There's no trouble. No fighting. No bomb. That's all that Klaus was looking for. He wanted a better world. Can you blame him?"

"Yes," said Crank.

Feynman said, "You're very young."

"I know what's right," said Crank.

Feynman's gaze moved to me. "At the restaurant, you asked Jerry a question. Remember?"

I nodded. "What if you look at the world and don't like what you see?"

"Well," said Feynman, "I don't see flying saucers, the way your friend does. There's no scientific proof. But you may be right about that other thing."

"What thing?" I asked.

"The world is full of monsters," he said. "Maybe I'm one of them."

13 · A LAND OF SHADOWS

THE GUARD FROWNED AT US. "YOU WANT TO GET INTO THE STUDIO?"

"We're friends of Laura Burke," I said.

He checked a list on his clipboard. "She hasn't come through yet. I'm not even sure she'll be here today."

Oz said, "We're going to watch them shoot a scene."

"I don't think so," said the guard.

"But we have to," said Arnie.

"Sorry," said the guard.

It was Wednesday, and we had gotten up early to catch the bus to Hollywood. At nine o'clock we had been at the front gate of Allied Artists, just as Laura had suggested. Now we wondered if we would ever get in.

As we turned away, a Ford convertible drove up to the gate. Don Siegel was driving. He spotted Oz and waved.

"So, you're back?" he called.

"Maybe not," said Oz. "We can't get in."

Siegel called the guard over and said a few words. The guard nodded. Siegel motioned us over.

"You boys are with me," he said. "Hop in."

We climbed into the backseat. As we drove past the guard, Crank thumbed his nose.

Inside the gate, Arnie glanced around. "Where's the studio?"

Siegel laughed. "You're looking at it."

It was like a town. There were streets lined with bungalows and office buildings. It had a post office and a restaurant, which Siegel called the commissary. A few cars drove the streets, along with golf carts and bicycles, but mostly people walked—chatting, checking scripts, pushing racks of clothing.

Oz asked Siegel, "Where's the soundstage?"

"Around the corner. But first I'm going to the screening room to see some dailies. Want to come?"

"Sure!" said Oz.

Siegel parked in front of a low building and took a round metal film can from the seat beside him. Oz, seeing Arnie's confusion, explained.

"At the end of each day, the crew takes the new scenes to the lab to be developed. They're called dailies."

Siegel led us into the building, down a hall, and through a door.

"Wow!" said Arnie as we walked inside. "Can I have one of these for my house?"

It was a movie theater, familiar in every detail except for the size. There was a projection booth, a screen, even a popcorn machine. But instead of hundreds of seats, there were just a few rows. Walter Wanger, the producer and Siegel's boss, sat near the front, deep in conversation with a dark-haired young man. I recognized him from one of the Sierra Madre scenes as the meter reader, Charlie.

"What are you doing here?" Siegel asked him.

The young man looked up. "I thought I might pick up a few tricks. You know, I'm going to make movies someday."

"God help us all," said Siegel. Turning to us, he explained, "That's Sam Peckinpah. He can't get enough of movies—kind of like you. Only difference is, instead of horror films, he goes for blood and guts."

"Westerns, too," said Peckinpah. "Hey, here's an idea. What if I made a Western with blood and guts?"

"Wonderful," said the director.

Siegel introduced us to Walter Wanger, then took the film can to the projectionist. When he came back, he settled in behind Wanger. I thought maybe we should sit in the back row, but Oz took us up front, like always. He said the colors were brighter there.

The lights dimmed. The projector started. And Oz got a surprise. There were no colors.

Miles examined the body on the pool table. Becky looked on nervously. Jack cut his hand and bled. Teddy screamed. And it all happened in black and white, in a land of shadows, a world very much like mine. There were odd angles, strange perspectives, and, beneath it all, a sense that something terrible was about to happen.

When the lights came back on, a man in a pin-striped suit stood by the door. His eyes were cold, and his face had a strange, unfinished look.

I whispered to Peckinpah, "Who's he?"

"Sherwin Gray, one of the studio executives. I've seen him around the set."

Walter Wanger rose to greet him. "Well, Sherwin, what did you think?"

Gray shook his head briskly. "Too scary."

Siegel stared at him. "It's a horror film. You're supposed to be scared."

"It seems real," said Gray. "The whole script is like that."

Siegel said, "Good. That means I'm doing my job."

"It's not us I'm worried about," said Gray. "It's the families, the kids. Ask these boys. You scared the life out of them."

I glanced at my friends. Arnie was hugging his knees. Crank gripped the armrests. Oz was as pale as a ghost. In other words, everything was fine.

"We like to be scared," I said.

"Nonsense," replied Gray. He turned to Wanger. "We need to change the ending."

Siegel jumped to his feet. "What do you mean? The ending's great. Miles looks into the camera and yells, 'They're here already! You're next!'"

"It's too much," said Gray. "You want people to believe it's true?"

"Of course!" Siegel said, "The lights come up, and a guy in the audience sneaks a peek at his girlfriend. Is she one of them?"

"Oh, God, is she?" asked Arnie.

"See?" said Siegel. "It's perfect."

"Change it," said Gray. "Tack on a new ending. The good guys win."

"How do they do that?" Siegel asked.

"I don't know. Bring in the police. Call the FBI. You figure it out."

Siegel glanced at Wanger, looking for help.

Wanger said, "It would hurt the picture, Sherwin. A new ending would water it down."

"With all due respect," said Gray, flashing an icy smile, "you're in no position to complain."

He stared at Wanger. A look passed between them that was sharp and painful. Wanger, wanting no part of it, dropped his gaze.

"Get your writer on it," said Gray. "Then show me the pages." He nodded curtly and left the room.

"What just happened?" asked Peckinpah.

Siegel eyed Wanger. "Hollywood happened. The big fish eat the little fish. The little fish eat the minnows. We're the minnows."

They decided to run the dailies again, and I had the same reaction as before. When the creature on the pool table opened its eyes, I felt a sudden urge to visit the bathroom.

I slipped out and went up the hall. As I did, I heard voices. I couldn't make out what they were saying, but I recognized one of them as Sherwin Gray's. Tiptoeing, I peered around the corner.

At the other end of the hall I saw two men deep in conversation. One of them was Gray. He was talking to Darryl Gibbons. Darryl had his notebook open, and the two of them seemed to be discussing something in it.

Why would a studio executive talk to an extra? He wouldn't. But he might talk to an FBI agent. Gray knew about Darryl; I was sure of it. Maybe Gray was the one who had called him in.

They finished their conversation and moved off down the hall. After they left, I continued on to the bathroom, then returned to the screening room. When I got there, the dailies were over and the lights were on. Siegel was talking to Wanger, but I could tell he wasn't getting anyplace. Siegel turned when he saw me.

"Welcome to the sausage factory," he said.

"Sausage factory?"

"That's what we're making here, right?" said Siegel, glancing at Wanger. "Grind 'em out, pack 'em up, throw 'em on a bun. They stink, but you won't notice if you use lots of mustard."

"It's the movie business," said Wanger.

"It's not art, I can tell you that," said Siegel.

"It never was," said Wanger.

The projectionist brought the dailies back to Siegel, who took the film can and left the building with Wanger, heading down the street toward the soundstage. Oz followed along, firing questions at Peckinpah. Behind them, Crank and Arnie continued the argument they had started on the day they met.

I was about to join them when I heard someone call my name. I turned and saw Laura, waving as she approached.

"Sorry about this morning," she said, out of breath. "Something came up. You know, business."

I wanted to ask what kind of business an actress would have before arriving at the studio but decided not to. Instead, I told her how Siegel had gotten us in and let us see the dailies. She seemed pleased but distracted.

"I should be going," she said, glancing at her watch. "I'm supposed to meet Carolyn Jones. See you later, okay?"

She drifted away, and I caught up with my friends as they approached the soundstage. It was a giant boxlike structure that might have been a warehouse, except most warehouses don't have aliens going in and out. There was a huge door on wheels, big enough to move cars and equipment through, as well as a smaller door for people, with a red light above it to show when the camera was rolling.

Siegel, Wanger, and Peckinpah went through the smaller door, and we were about to follow when Crank spotted Darryl chatting with an actress outside. Darryl shot her a big grin, watched her leave, then jotted down something in his notebook. Crank approached, and we reluctantly followed.

"How's the case going?" Crank asked him.

Darryl quickly put away his notebook. "Hey, keep it down, will you?"

"We won't tell anyone," said Crank.

I expected Darryl to discourage Crank, but he didn't. He looked around to see if anyone was listening, then got a sneaky little smile on his face. It occurred to me that Darryl liked having someone to share his secrets with who admired him and wanted to hear how clever he was.

"I've been investigating the unions," he said in a low voice. "It's starting to look like someone in the cast is a link to the Communists."

"You know what I heard?" said Oz. "There's a plot to steal the pods and dye them pink."

Darryl glared at him. "You think this is a joke? It's real. Ask J. Edgar Hoover."

"The people we've met seem nice enough," said Oz. "Right, guys?"

Arnie and I nodded. Darryl shook his head in disgust. "You can't judge people by the way they act. You have to investigate, check them out. Everyone has secrets. If you dig, you'll find them."

I thought of Oz's father, hiding in the bedroom. I thought of my own family and the things we didn't say.

"What kind of secrets?" I asked.

Darryl glanced around. "Take that guy Sam Peckinpah. He's obsessed with violence."

Oz said, "That's no secret. It was practically the first thing he told me."

"Well, then there's Wanger," said Darryl.

I pictured Walter Wanger, cool and elegant. "What about him?" I asked.

"Did you ever wonder why he's working on a low-budget picture like this?"

"Maybe because it's good," said Arnie.

Darryl snorted. "It's strictly a B movie. Second tier. Low class. Did you know he used to be one of the highest-paid producers in town? In 1942 he made nine hundred thousand dollars, more than anyone in Hollywood except Louis B. Mayer."

I could tell even Oz was impressed by that.

Darryl continued, "He had his own distribution company. Made some big pictures too. He married Joan Bennett, the actress. Then, four years ago, it happened."

"What?" asked Arnie.

"He got mad at his wife's agent. So he pulled a gun and shot him. The agent lived, but Wanger went to prison."

I stared at him. "Walter Wanger was in prison?"

"Think about it," said Darryl. "What film did he produce right before this one?"

Oz said, "*Riot in Cell Block Eleven*. He did it with Don Siegel."

"Probably the most realistic prison film ever made," said Darryl. "Now you know why."

We looked at each other, stunned.

Darryl said, "When Wanger was released from prison, no one would touch him. Finally he got a break. There was a call from Sherwin Gray at Allied Artists, offering him a B movie. Now the great Walter Wanger does prison stories and horror films."

I didn't like Darryl's story, but it made sense. For one thing, it explained what I'd seen on Wanger's face in the screening room when Gray had challenged him. It was fear.

We entered the soundstage and saw Siegel huddled with the actors. Behind him was the set—a stairway, with a phone on a small table. There were pictures on the wall and flowers in a vase. When the cameras rolled, Miles and Becky hurried to call the police, reporting pods in basements all around town.

It was a horror film, but it was more than that. Beneath the surface, beyond the studio walls, something dangerous was taking shape. As the world slept, it quietly moved into place, waiting.

14 · THE LETTER

ON THE BUS HOME THAT AFTERNOON, CRANK CONVINCED US TO STOP AT CAL TECH TO CHECK ON FEYNMAN. As we crossed the campus, we noticed an unexpected sound. Someone was playing bongo drums.

The drummer was pouring his heart into the music. He was angry, joyful, hopeful. In the end, he was sad. We followed the sound, and it led us to Feynman's office.

When the playing stopped, Crank tapped on the door. Richard Feynman opened it, holding a set of bongos. He eyed us warily. "I can't seem to get rid of you, can I?"

"We didn't mean to bother you," said Oz. "We can go if you want."

Feynman shrugged. "It's all right. Come on in."

He set the bongos in the corner and flopped down in his desk chair. Oz, Arnie, and I perched on the shabby sofa. Crank stood, shifting uneasily, his eyes roaming around the room.

"You're good with those drums," said Arnie.

Feynman smiled sadly. "I can't carry a tune, but I do have rhythm. As a kid, I was always tapping my foot or keeping time with the silverware. Drove my parents crazy. I guess I never stopped."

I remembered what Zorthian had said about science and art. "Maybe you're looking for the truth," I said.

He shook his head. "Drumming isn't a search for the truth. It's what you do when you know you'll never find it." He gestured at a blackboard beside his desk. "See those equations? They're wasted, all of them. They lead nowhere. When I get sick of it all, I pick up my bongos. I drum so I can make it through the day."

There was a knock at the door. When Feynman opened it, I recognized Mulligan, the student we'd met in his class that first day.

Seeing us, Mulligan nodded, then said to Feynman, "Remember those questions you told us to write? I'm having trouble with one of them."

"Oh, yeah?" said Feynman. "Which one?"

Mulligan shot us an uneasy glance. He asked Feynman, "Can you come outside for a minute?"

"Huh? Sure, I guess." Feynman looked back at us.

"Go ahead," said Crank. "We're fine."

Feynman went outside to talk with Mulligan. As the door swung shut, Crank eyed the photo of Klaus Fuchs, then moved to Feynman's bookshelf.

"What are you doing?" I asked.

Crank tilted his head, scanning the book titles. "Looking for clues." He moved to the desk, where he examined some papers that were scattered on top.

Oz jumped to his feet. "Those things are private."

"Oh my God," said Crank. He reached for a letter that lay open on top of the desk, but Oz grabbed his arm before he could pick it up.

Oz said, "You can't touch that. It doesn't belong to you."

Brushing Oz away like a mosquito, Crank picked up the letter.

"What is it?" asked Arnie.

Crank grinned. "It may be the smoking gun."

Oz tried to take it away. Crank held him off with one hand. With the other he showed Arnie and me the letter.

```
EMBASSY OF THE UNION OF SOVIET
SOCIALIST REPUBLICS
Washington, D.C.


January 10, 1955


Professor Richard Phillips Feynman
California Institute of Technology
Pasadena, California


Dear Professor Feynman:
    The Academy of Sciences of the USSR
has asked me to convey to you the
```

invitation of the Academy to take part
in the All-Union Conference on the
Quantum Theory of Electrodynamics and
the Theory of Elementary Particles which
will be held by the Academy of Sciences
in Moscow from April 30 to May 6.

The Academy will take care of all
expenses connected with your stay in
the Soviet Union.

A letter containing the invitation
and a preliminary program of the
conference has been sent to you by Air
Mail directly from Moscow.

I shall be grateful to you if you
will let me know whether you will
accept the invitation of the Academy of
Sciences of the USSR.

Sincerely yours,
Georgi N. Zaroubin
Ambassador of the Soviet Union to the USA

As we finished reading, the doorknob rattled.

"He's coming back!" said Arnie.

Moving quickly, Crank replaced the letter and stepped
away from the desk. The rest of us scurried to our seats on the
sofa. Somehow Oz ended up in Arnie's lap.

Luckily, Feynman didn't notice. When he came back in, he was thoughtful. "Well, Mulligan really did need help with a question. Want to know what it was?"

We nodded.

"How come the girls don't like me?"

Arnie stared at Feynman. "Really? The girls don't like you?"

Crank punched him on the arm. "Not Feynman, you idiot. Mulligan. That's why he was embarrassed."

Feynman chuckled. "I told him to keep trying. They'll come around. And if it doesn't work, then do what I do."

"What's that?" I asked.

Feynman reached over, picked up the bongos, and beat out a mournful rhythm.

"Play the drums," he said.

"Do you still believe he's innocent?" asked Crank.

It was later that night, and Oz had invited us to eat at his house. I had expected my mother to say no, since she liked having me home for dinner. This time, though, she agreed, sounding almost relieved. It worried me. Why didn't she want me home? What was going on?

At Oz's house, I was quiet during dinner. Bernice didn't seem to notice. She was too busy ranting about the curse of modern life, plastic. Next to her, Maury picked at his food, glancing at us warily. He wasn't wearing pajamas anymore, but his clothes were so wrinkled I wondered if he'd been sleeping in them.

After dinner Bernice went off to run some errands. We went to Oz's room and shut the door. That was when Crank asked us about Feynman.

"Of course he's innocent," said Oz.

Arnie said, "What about the letter?"

"That's obvious," said Crank. "We need to show it to Darryl."

Oz sat up straight. "We can't do that!"

I put a hand on his shoulder. "It's okay. Just relax."

"It's not okay," he said, pushing away my hand. "That letter's private property."

Crank leaned toward Oz and pronounced his words carefully, as if dealing with a slow learner. "It's from the Russians. Maybe you've heard of them? They want to destroy our way of life."

"They're holding a conference," said Oz. "Big deal."

Crank stared in disbelief. "Did you see what they'll be talking about? Quantum theory and elementary particles. It's about the atomic bomb, and they want Feynman there."

Arnie said, "It does seem suspicious."

"Feynman plays the drums when he's feeling bad," said Crank. "No wonder the guy's depressed. He's betraying his country."

"Guys," I said. "Come on, now."

"He's not a traitor!" said Oz. "He's just doing his job."

Crank said, "Like your grandfather?"

Oz glared at him. "Yeah. Want to make something of it?"

"Let's see," said Crank, "what party did your grandfather belong to? Was it the Democrats? the Republicans?"

"He was a Communist," said Oz.

Crank got to his feet and strolled around the room. "Did you guys ever notice how many things Oz has that are red? It's his favorite color."

I said, "Cut it out, both of you."

Crank gestured at Oz. "He's always talking about the United Nations. What about the United States? In all the time we've been coming to his house, have you ever seen an American flag?"

Oz sprang to his feet. "You're a jerk, you know that?"

Crank took two quick steps toward him. I slid in between them, trying to hold them apart. "Just calm down," I said.

Crank reached over me, trying to get at him. "What did you call me?"

Oz glared up at him, defiant. "Nazi jerk."

With a roar, Crank launched himself at Oz, going up and over me. He grabbed Oz, and the three of us sprawled on the floor, with Crank on top, Oz on the bottom, and me in the middle, trying desperately to keep them apart.

"Guys!" I yelled. "Please!"

Arnie jumped onto Crank's back. Swatting him away, Crank shoved me aside and hammered Oz in the stomach.

Oz gasped, his face flushed, and untangled himself from the pile. Stumbling to his feet, he pointed at Crank. "Get out!"

"What's wrong?" asked Crank. "Can't stand the truth?"

"Get out of my house," Oz said. "I mean it."

Crank gazed at Oz, then shook his head. "My pleasure."

He pulled himself up, yanked open the door, and stomped out of the bedroom. Oz followed to make sure he really left. A moment later, I heard the front door slam.

When Oz came back, his face was still red. I told him, "It's okay. It'll be fine."

"Stop it," said Oz.

I glanced at him. "Huh?"

"Just stop it. You're always trying to smooth things over."

Arnie said, "Don't get mad at Paul. He was trying to help."

"He's making it worse," said Oz. He went over to his bed and stretched out, staring at the ceiling.

I thought about what he had said. Maybe I really was making things worse. My father was always mad. My parents didn't get along. My family was coming apart. Now my friends were too. Wherever I went, there was trouble. Whatever I tried, things got worse.

Arnie said, "We're still friends, aren't we?"

"Not with Crank," said Oz. "I hate him."

I said, "No, you don't."

Oz looked at me and shook his head. "Grow up," he said.

15 · ALIENS IN T-SHIRTS

I HAVE A CONFESSION TO MAKE. I'M A POD PERSON.

At least, I was for a few minutes. It happened in Beachwood Canyon, near Griffith Park.

After our conversation at Oz's house, Arnie, Oz, and I had agreed to meet in Sierra Madre the next day to catch the bus into Hollywood. On my way home that night, I had stopped by Crank's place to let him know. Crank's mom had said he wasn't home yet but had promised to give him the message.

When we got to the bus stop the next morning, Crank wasn't there. He still hadn't arrived when the bus pulled in.

"What if something happened to him?" asked Arnie, his forehead bunched up.

Oz said, "It's not Crank I'm worried about. It's the letter."

"What do you mean?" asked Arnie.

"Remember what he said? He wanted to show Feynman's letter to Darryl."

I stared at him. "You really think he'd do that?"

"Did you see the look on his face?" Oz asked. "He thinks he's in some kind of movie. *Eugene Crookshank, Secret Agent*."

"Hey, you kids," called the bus driver through the open door. "Are you getting on or not?"

"Let's go," I said. "He'll turn up." I said it, but I wasn't sure I believed it.

We took the bus to Beachwood Canyon, one of several streets that snaked through the Hollywood Hills, where the day's shooting was supposed to take place. When we got off the bus, it wasn't hard to tell where the location was. The mouth of the canyon was crowded with cars. Among them, I saw Siegel's Ford convertible and Laura's blue Plymouth sedan.

We walked past the cars and into the canyon. Around us, the hills rose steeply on both sides. Amazingly, the canyon was filled with houses, many of them perched on what looked like stilts. Between two of the houses was a stone stairway that reached from the street to the top of the hill, with iron railings on either side. The crew was clustered around the stairway. We moved closer to see what was going on.

Halfway up the stairs, Don Siegel was huddled with the cameraman, Ellsworth Fredericks, and several crew members.

"What are they doing?" asked Arnie.

Behind us a familiar voice said, "They're setting up the shot."

We turned around, and there was Laura. I realized that, as

excited as I was to be on a movie location, she was the person I had come to see.

"Remember how the pod people chased Miles and Becky up the street in Sierra Madre?" she said. "This is the next shot. They try to escape by running up the stairway and over the hill."

Oz studied Siegel and the crew. "What's that thing on the railings?"

It looked like a railroad cart, with wheels that rode the railings and a wooden platform in between.

"Clever, isn't it?" she said. "The head grip rigged up a special dolly for the camera, so it can roll up the stairway ahead of the actors and shoot down at them."

As we watched, Fredericks and a crew member lifted a camera onto the platform and secured it with belts. With the other crew members helping, they tried dollying up and down the stairway. Fredericks, moving with the camera, peered through the eyepiece. He said something to Siegel, who nodded and turned to the rest of the crew.

"Let's move it, people! Time is money."

The crew scattered, and a crowd of extras gathered at the base of the stairway.

"I'd better go," said Laura. "The pods are calling."

As she moved off, Siegel brushed by. He saw Oz and grinned.

"What do you think of our dolly?"

"Nice," said Oz.

Siegel glanced down at the extras, then back at us. "You know," he said, "we need a big crowd for this shot. You boys wouldn't want to be in it, would you?"

And that's how I became a pod person.

When you watch the movie, you'll see a crowd of people chasing Miles and Becky up the stairway. Laura, her face blank and expressionless, is one of them. Behind her, if you look carefully, you can spot three aliens in T-shirts and jeans.

I can tell you, acting is a hard job. We must have run up that stairway twenty times, with Fredericks and the crew doing each take a little differently. There was a street at the top of the stairs, where at the end of each take Siegel would talk to the extras. His instructions were simple.

"Stop trying to act! You're not angry. You're not sad. You're zombies. You look like people, but you're dead inside."

On about the tenth take, I began to wonder if it was true. My family was in trouble. So were my friends. My world was falling apart. Meanwhile, the bomb could drop any minute. There was danger. There were tough choices to make. And what did I do? I just moved up and down the stairs, going nowhere, my eyes glazed over and my mind blank. Maybe I really was dead inside.

It took most of the day, but finally Siegel got the shot he wanted. Afterward Laura turned to us. "I'm starved! Let's go to Musso & Frank's."

Musso & Frank's Grill on Hollywood Boulevard was a favorite hangout for movie people. We had stuck our heads inside a few times but had never worked up the courage to eat there. The idea of going there with Laura made my heart pound. But she wasn't the only thing on my mind.

"I'm worried about Crank," I said.

"I have to get home," said Arnie. "I'll stop by his house on the way."

I said, "Really? Could you?"

Oz studied Laura and me. "I need to be going too. Come on, Arnie, I'll keep you company."

And just like that, I was alone with Laura Burke.

The restaurant had booths with leather seats and wood-paneled walls, the perfect place for dinner with a future star. I watched Laura glance at the menu, and it occurred to me that she wasn't much older than I was. What was ten years in the scheme of things? It might seem like a lot now, but when I was thirty and she was forty, who would care?

She ordered a salad, explaining that she was watching her weight. I got a hamburger and told her about growing up in Sierra Madre. I admitted that it had been pretty boring until she and her friends had arrived. Until then, most of the excitement had come on weekends, when Crank, Arnie, Oz, and I had gone to horror movies. As I described our trips, she gave me a funny look.

"You enjoy being scared?"

"I don't know if *enjoy* is the right word," I said. "It feels right. It seems familiar."

She asked what my family was like. I described my mother and sister and the way my father glared at me as if I had committed a crime.

Laura nodded thoughtfully and listened. I couldn't remember the last time my parents had listened to me the way she did. I tried to recall a conversation between them. How long had it been since they had really talked to each other? They were trapped together, and I was trapped with them. Maybe with Laura I'd find a way to escape.

"What about you?" I asked. "Where are you from?"

"Richmond, Indiana. It's a little town near Indianapolis."

"How did you end up in Hollywood?"

"It doesn't matter," she said.

"Come on," I said, "you can tell me."

She picked at her salad. Finally, she said, "When you watch people in a movie, they seem perfect—the lighting, the hair, the makeup. But it's all a trick. We're not the way we seem. You know that, don't you?"

"Yeah, I guess."

She studied my face, then put her hand on mine. It tingled where she touched me. "I like you."

"I like you, too," I said.

Her eyes looked sad. I wanted to ask her why, but something told me not to.

"I'm not the person you think I am," she said.

I remembered what Darryl had said. Everyone has secrets. What were hers?

"Can I help you?" asked the lady at the register.

My father looked around nervously to see if anyone was listening. "Do you have little bunny decorations? You know, the kind that go on cookies and cakes?"

It was Thursday night. I had come home from Musso & Frank's to find my mother and Lulu baking cookies. They were halfway through mixing the dough when Lulu decided she wanted bunny cookies. Since she and my mother were busy, Lulu asked my father if he would go to the store and get some decorations. Luckily for her, the only thing that held more power over my father than the TV was Lulu's lower lip.

The lady barely looked up. "Aisle nine, baked goods."

I followed him in that direction, reading the latest issue of *Amazing Stories*. As we made our way down the aisle, I bumped into a shopping cart and looked up to see Mrs. Kramer.

"Paul!" she said. "What are you doing here?"

I shrugged. "Reading, mostly."

It was strange seeing a teacher at the grocery. She was wearing jeans and loafers, almost like a regular person.

"So, is this your father?" she asked.

He stood nearby, eyeing her warily. I nodded. "Dad, this is Mrs. Kramer. She's my social studies teacher."

"Please," she told him, extending her hand, "I'm Millicent."

Millicent?

"I'm Gerald," he said. He took her hand awkwardly, as if he didn't know whether to shake it or change the channel. Meanwhile I noticed the groceries in her cart—hamburger buns, a bag of charcoal, five cans of lighter fluid.

She saw me looking and grinned. "You can never have too much lighter fluid, I always say. We're having a cookout tonight. What could be more American, right?"

I said, "Yeah, I guess."

"You soak the charcoal in fluid—I mean really soak it—then you stand back, light a match, and toss it on the pile. Boom! It's great."

"I like burgers," I said.

"Burgers?" she said. "Oh, yeah, they're okay. How about you, Gerald? What's on your grocery list?"

My father mumbled something.

"Sorry, what was that?" asked Mrs. Kramer.

"Bunny decorations," he said.

"The kind you put on cookies," I explained.

Nodding, she raised her eyebrows. "Cool."

We stood there for a minute, wondering who would talk next.

"So, Gerald," she said, "I hear you work at Lockheed."

He glanced at me accusingly. I said, "She asked me in class."

"Funny thing was," said Mrs. Kramer, "Paul didn't know what you do there. Just told me you work on planes."

My father looked around, maybe checking for exits.

I said, "His job is kind of a secret."

Mrs. Kramer rubbed her hands together. "A secret? I love it. What kind of planes?"

He shifted uncomfortably. "I'd rather not say."

She poked him with her elbow. "Come on, Gerald, you can tell me. You're among friends."

My father's face started to turn red. He wasn't just embarrassed. He was getting mad. Mrs. Kramer didn't notice.

"You and all the other defense workers, you're the real heroes," she told him.

His face got redder.

"You're the soldiers of the cold war," she said.

I shifted nervously. "Well, I guess we should be going," I said.

She tossed my father a wink. "How about a hint? Can you spell *nuclear*?"

His eyes narrowed. I could see it coming—the Look. Mrs. Kramer would be burned to a crisp, zapped like the priest in *The War of the Worlds*.

I grabbed some decorations from the shelf. "We don't want those cookies to get cold. Right, Dad? Let's go."

Taking my father's arm, I pulled him toward the checkout line. "Great seeing you, Mrs. Kramer. Good luck with your fluids."

A few minutes later we were in the car. My father sat behind the wheel, his jaw working.

"Are you all right?" I asked.

"I'm not a hero," he said. *"I am not a hero!"*

He pounded the steering wheel. The horn blared. An old man gaped at us, then hugged his grocery bag and hurried away.

"It's okay," I said. "You don't have to talk about it."

"Yes, I do." He gritted his teeth when he said it. His voice was hoarse. His face, usually blank, rippled with emotion. He was fighting a battle. Something inside of him was trying to get out.

"I never wanted that job," he managed finally.

"At Lockheed?"

He nodded, struggling to speak. "I was back from the war, looking for work. I wanted to get as far away from the army as I could. I was sick of watching people die." There was a catch in his voice.

I wanted to tell him it was all right, but I didn't know what to say.

He took a ragged breath. "But I was broke, with a wife and a three-year-old son. That's when an army friend called. He offered me a job doing what I'd done in the war."

"Working on planes?" I asked.

He crossed his arms, shivering. "I didn't want to, but it was good money. So I went along. We made bombers. First for regular bombs and then . . ." He took a deep breath. "Finally I couldn't take it anymore. I decided to quit. When I got home that night, your mother told me she was pregnant. We needed a bigger house and car. I didn't have a choice."

He closed his eyes and shook his head. A look of pain flashed across his face. Finally he stopped and sat very still. When he opened his eyes a moment later, his expression was blank. The struggle was over. "So I stayed. And here I am. Nice house. Good car. The perfect life."

"Don't say that," I told him. "You could get another job."

Something flickered behind his eyes. I was surprised when I realized what it was. It wasn't anger, or even regret. It was fear.

"Yeah, sure," he said. "Sell the house, get an apartment, eat macaroni and cheese."

"But you're not happy."

He gave me a weary smile. "We have a nice TV, don't we?"

Later that night I watched him stare at his beautiful TV, and I thought of all the people who were afraid. It wasn't just me. It was my father. It was Mr. Feldman. It was Laura and Walter Wanger and the people in my class crouching under their desks. Maybe the question isn't whether you're afraid, but what you do about it. You can push the fear aside and pretend it isn't there. You can smooth it over, hoping it goes away. Or you can face it and try to do the right thing, even if it hurts.

My father sat alone in his chair. Shadows flickered across his face. Across the room, in black and white, someone was talking. Someone laughed. He barely noticed.

16 · DON'T FALL ASLEEP

MILES AND BECKY SCRAMBLED THROUGH THE CANYONS, TRYING TO ESCAPE. Behind them came the pod people. Becky stumbled and fell. Miles picked her up in his arms. Looking around desperately, he saw a cave and carried her inside, where they rested against the wall.

Becky gasped, "Miles, I can't. I can't go on."

"Yes, you can."

Miles noticed a hole in the floor of the cave, covered by boards. He and Becky climbed inside and pulled the boards over them just in time. The pod people came streaming into the cave. Charlie the meter reader called, "Give up! You can't get away from us." But they didn't find the hiding place.

After the pod people left, Miles and Becky climbed out. They splashed water on their faces to stay awake, then Miles went outside to look for help. When he came back, he lifted Becky and carried her to the mouth of the cave. He slipped, and as the two of them lay there, he leaned down to kiss her.

Her eyes popped open. She stared up at him. He gasped.

In a flat, expressionless voice she said, "I went to sleep, and it happened."

"I should never have left you," he moaned.

"Stop acting like a fool, Miles, and accept us."

He shook his head. "No. Never!"

Becky screamed, "He's in here! He's in here! Get him!"

Where do you find a cave in Hollywood?

As it turned out, the answer was simple. In Griffith Park, next to Beachwood Canyon, was a rock quarry that had been abandoned in the early 1900s. In it was a series of caves and tunnels. Somewhere along the line, Hollywood had discovered the quarry and had begun using it as a movie location. Oz explained that the area, known as Bronson Canyon, had been in dozens of films, including *Lost Horizon*, *The Adventures of Captain Marvel*, and *The Three Musketeers*. It had seen cowboys and Indians, pirates, knights, pioneers, and every kind of monster. To me, the monster that used to be Becky was the scariest of all.

By the time they finished the scene, it was after five o'clock. Oz, Arnie, and I walked out of the quarry, heading for the bus stop.

"There's Crank!" said Arnie, pointing toward a parking lot by the road.

While Laura and I had been at Musso & Frank's the day before, Arnie and Oz had looked for Crank. They hadn't found him, but his mother had told them he was fine and would be at the movie location the following day. Now here he was, except for one problem.

"He's with Darryl," said Oz, frowning.

The two of them stood beside Darryl's black Plymouth, talking. Arnie waved.

"Hey, Crank!" He ran to join them. Oz and I followed along behind.

"Where have you been?" Arnie asked Crank when he caught up.

"Busy," Crank said, grinning.

"You missed a chance to be in the movie," said Arnie. He described the scene on the stairway the previous day and the special dolly the crew had built.

"I didn't need a movie," said Crank. "I had the real thing." He looked over at Darryl, who shot us a tight smile.

"Thanks for the tip, guys," Darryl said. "You've done your country a real service."

Arnie beamed. "Sure, any time."

Oz eyed Darryl suspiciously. "What did we do?"

"You found the letter," he said. "It's dynamite. Or maybe I should say, it's a bomb."

I stared at Crank. "You told him about the letter?"

"Somebody had to," said Crank.

Darryl said, "I know about all of it—the photo with Fuchs, the car, the locks, the safe, the suspicious friends. In fact, I've done a little digging on my own. It seems that when Feynman was at Los Alamos, he wrote messages in code. Why would he do that?"

"Maybe he likes games," said Oz.

"I'll tell you another game he liked," said Darryl. "Los Alamos was a top-secret base, with chain-link fences and military guards. He used to sneak out by crawling under the fence. The guy was a security nightmare waiting to happen. Now it's happened."

Oz said, "He's a college professor. He helps students. He's not a spy."

"That's what I thought for a while," said Darryl. "Seeing the letter changed my mind."

"Wait a second," said Oz. "How did you see it? It's in Feynman's office."

I whirled and faced Crank. "Did you break in?"

Crank snorted. "We didn't have to. He keeps the door unlocked, remember?"

"You went inside and stole it?"

Darryl said, "Of course not. We wouldn't do that." He reached into his pocket and pulled out the spy camera. "We took a picture."

Crank said, "I don't think Feynman will be teaching much longer."

I stared at him. "That was wrong. You shouldn't have done it."

"I'll develop the picture tonight," said Darryl. "My boss is going to love it. So will J. Edgar Hoover."

I glanced at the camera, no bigger than a cigarette lighter. It was hard to believe that it contained enough information to ruin a man's career.

Darryl put the camera away and looked at his watch. "I should get going. It'll be a busy night."

As he turned to leave, I thought of Richard Feynman. Feynman had trusted us. He had let us into his office and had told us what he was working on. All the while, we were spying on him. We had thought we were helping our country, but were we really?

I remembered the fear in my father's eyes. I thought I could see it in Darryl's. Why else would he sneak around, investigating actors and college professors? It was like a sickness, spreading from Washington to Sierra Madre, from J. Edgar Hoover to Darryl, from Mrs. Kramer to Arnie, Crank, Oz, and me. If it's new, doubt it. If it's different, stamp it out. If you don't understand it, destroy it. Miles Bennell saw what could happen. Now I did too.

Sometime tonight, Darryl would make a call that could ruin Richard Feynman. We had caused it, and we were the only ones who could stop him. Thinking about it, a chill snaked up my spine. It was the same feeling I had every Saturday at the movies, but this time it was real. I was afraid.

I could give in to the fear and keep my mouth shut, the way my father had. After all, we were just a bunch of thirteen-year-old kids up against the FBI. Or I could fight back. It might be stupid. It might get me into trouble. I might even get hurt. But I would know that I had tried.

I looked at the camera and had an idea. "Hey, Darryl," I said, "how about some ice cream?"

By the time we got to C. C. Brown's, I had described every item on the menu in mouth-watering detail. When we went inside, it was all we could do to keep Darryl from diving over the counter and into the freezer.

His first sundae, Mocha Madness, had three scoops of coffee ice cream topped with chocolate syrup and walnuts. His second, Dieter's Revenge, featured hot fudge on chocolate ice cream with cookies. As he worked on his third, a banana ice cream with brownies and whipped cream, called Gorilla's Treat, I asked him about the camera.

"I can't believe it actually takes pictures," I said. "Can I see it again?"

Darryl looked up, his mouth smeared with chocolate sauce. Reaching into his pocket, he handed me the camera.

I studied the tiny device, squinting to make out the features. "The light's not very good here," I said. "I'll be right back."

I headed toward the big front window, which happened to be right next to the door. When I got there, I turned to the others and gave a quick nod. It was a signal that Arnie, Oz, and I had agreed on while huddled in the backseat of Darryl's car on the way over.

As Darryl plunged once more into the Gorilla's Treat,

Arnie and Oz got up and began walking toward me.

"Hey, where are you going?" asked Crank.

They kept walking. When they reached me, I tucked the camera into my pocket, and the three of us bolted out the door. We raced down Hollywood Boulevard, dodging tourists and pedestrians. We had the camera! In planning our move, we had thought about opening the camera to expose the film, but it had seemed important to save the photo so we could show what Darryl had done.

I glanced over my shoulder. Crank and Darryl hadn't come out of C. C. Brown's yet. Maybe Darryl, lost in his sundae, had been slow to realize what was happening. Maybe the waitress was asking them about the check.

As usual, there was a crowd in front of Grauman's Chinese Theater, where all the big stars in Hollywood had left handprints and signatures in the concrete. Looking for cover, I dove in among the people, with Oz and Arnie behind me. We picked our way through, past impressions of Marilyn Monroe's shoes, Jimmy Durante's nose, and the hoofprints of Roy Rogers's horse, Trigger. When we came out the other side, Darryl and Crank were just emerging from C. C. Brown's.

"I have an idea," I said.

The traffic light turned green, and we sprinted across the street to one place where, if we were lucky, they would never think to look.

"Hello, sir," I said as we breezed into Frederick's of Hollywood.

The manager stared at us.

"We're not here to buy anything," I explained.

"Yeah," said Arnie, "we're just browsing."

Oz said, "It's a matter of national security."

The manager pointed to the door. "Get out!" he bellowed.

"Hey," said Arnie, looking through some of the underwear, "what are these?"

I glanced past him at the front window just as Darryl and Crank hurried by, their heads swiveling. I had been right. They never thought to look inside. It was a perfect hiding place. Unfortunately, the manager disagreed.

A moment later, we were back on the street. Down the sidewalk, Darryl's head swiveled again, and this time he saw us.

"Move it!" I told the others.

The traffic light was red, but we crossed, anyway. Dodging cars and a city bus, somehow we reached the other side. We ducked into Pickwick Bookshop, ran through the aisles, and pounded up the stairs to the second level.

"Coming through," I said.

Readers scattered in front of us as we headed for a far corner of the shop. On the shelf was a sign: MAPS. Reaching it, I found what I was looking for—a book of Los Angeles bus routes. Quickly, I thumbed through it.

"Got it!" I said. "The number eight bus. We catch it at Vine."

There was a back door that we used sometimes as a

shortcut to the bus stop. Slamming through it, we hurried down an alley and up Vine Street.

Luck was on our side. The number 8 bus was just pulling in. As we climbed on, Darryl and Crank rounded the corner and spotted us.

We paid the fare and made our way to the last row of the bus, where I looked out the rear window. There was no sign of Darryl and Crank. When I turned back, Arnie was watching me.

"You seem different," he said.

I thought about it and smiled. Maybe I was.

A few minutes later, the black Plymouth appeared, passing cars like mad, trying to catch up. Arnie yelled to the bus driver, "How fast does this thing go?"

I said, "You know, I'm pretty sure we can't outrun them."

"Where are we going?" asked Oz.

"To Griffith Park," I said. "I was hoping we could get off there, but I didn't know Darryl and Crank would be behind us."

Oz said, "If we do, they'll see us. We'll never get away."

"Give me a minute," I said. "I'll think of something."

"My stomach hurts," said Arnie.

I sat up straight. "That's it!" Leaning over, I whispered instructions to them, then said, "Come on, Arnie, we're going to the front of the bus. Get ready to sneak out the door."

Arnie said, "How are we supposed to do that?"

"You'll see," I said.

Arnie and I moved to the front and took seats by the door, watching Oz all the while. As the bus passed Griffith Park, Oz moved over next to the rear stairwell, then doubled over.

"My stomach!" he screeched, collapsing into the stairwell.

"Hey," called one of the passengers, "somebody's hurt back here!"

The bus driver, a burly woman, glanced into the rearview mirror and saw a crowd forming at the stairwell. She jerked the wheel to one side, pulled over, and put on the emergency brake.

"Air!" wailed Oz. "I need air! I'm suffocating!"

"Open the door!" someone yelled.

The driver pulled a lever, and both sets of doors swung open. When they did, Oz went tumbling out the back. Some passengers stepped off the bus and gathered around him at the curb, where they were joined by the driver. A group of pedestrians craned their necks, trying to see what was happening.

"Now!" I murmured to Arnie. "Go!"

"We can't!" he said. "Oz is hurt!"

I grabbed Arnie's arm and yanked, dragging him down the steps, out the front door, and behind a big tree. Peering around it, I saw the Plymouth pull up behind the bus. As Darryl and Crank got out, a small figure broke through the crowd and went sprinting down the sidewalk in the other direction.

"It's Oz!" said Arnie.

The crowd gaped at him. The bus driver yelled. Darryl shouted something to Crank, then they took off after him.

As the people climbed back on the bus, Arnie and I slipped away. Crossing the street, we made our way up the road and into Griffith Park.

For my plan to work, we needed a place to hide for an hour or so. I knew the perfect spot.

17 · THE HUMANS AGAINST THE PODS

WE HURRIED THROUGH THE PARK, RETRACING OUR STEPS FROM EARLIER THAT DAY. By the time we reached Bronson Canyon, the sun had dipped below the trees, and the rock quarry was riddled with shadows.

"This place is creepy," said Arnie.

"Maybe so," I said, "but it's safe. No one comes here unless they're filming."

We rounded a corner, and there, like the empty sockets of a skull, were the caves.

Arnie laughed nervously. "Are there pod people inside?"

"You've seen too many horror movies," I said.

He grinned up at me, trying to look brave. "There's no such thing as too many horror movies."

I clapped him on the shoulder, and we approached the entrance to the main cave. As we peered inside, there was an explosion of sound, and a black cloud hurtled toward us.

Arnie screamed, "Look out!"

We dove for the ground. As the cloud sped by, it grazed my hair and gave off a faint sour smell.

"What was that?" said Arnie.

I turned and looked. The cloud broke into a hundred fragments, black against the sky.

"Bats," I said. "They like cool, dark places."

We edged inside the cave. Once our eyes adjusted, we could see what it looked like. The space, blasted and chiseled out sometime in the last century, was more like a tunnel than a cave. It extended for thirty yards, beyond which was a back entrance. Discarded cups and papers littered the floor, probably from the day's shoot.

"I guess they never learned to clean up their rooms," I joked, trying desperately to sound normal.

Arnie looked around. "Now what do we do?"

"We wait. We're not supposed to meet Oz for another hour."

"What if he doesn't get away?"

"He'll get away," I said, sounding more confident than I felt.

Sitting down, I leaned against the same wall where Miles and Becky had huddled. Arnie flopped down beside me. He started to whimper, "I'm—"

"I know. You're scared."

"How did you guess?"

"Look, Arnie, this time it's okay to be scared. This is serious stuff. It's about the bomb. We're up against the FBI."

Arnie shot me an odd little smile. "The humans against the pods. Just like in the movie."

As the sun sank lower in the sky, the cave cooled off. We sat in silence, and the gray walls darkened. On the way into the park we had bought sandwiches at a little market. Now we pulled them out and ate them. I hadn't realized how hungry I had been.

In between bites, Arnie said, "Is he really a spy?"

"Feynman? I don't think so."

"You have to admit, it does seem suspicious," said Arnie. "You know—the letter, the code, the locks. What about the picture of Klaus Fuchs? And how about the car?"

In spite of everything, part of me wanted to agree. It was the part that hated questions, that avoided trouble, that liked things nice and easy. It lived in the basement, ready to open its eyes if I fell asleep.

Shaking myself, I told Arnie, "You've got to be strong. Don't give in."

As we finished our sandwiches, I took the camera from my pocket and cradled it in my palm. Gripping it tightly, I pressed it against my chest. The light faded. Soon, Arnie was just a silhouette.

There were footsteps in the distance. A voice said, "You really think they're in there?"

It was Crank.

"You have any better ideas?" said Darryl. "The other one ran off at the bus stop."

Arnie gripped my arm. His hand was shaking. I glanced around the cave. There was no place to hide.

"We could go out the back," I whispered.

Then I noticed the boards. The movie crew had left them on the floor of the cave, covering the hole where Miles and Becky had hidden from the pod people. Arnie, Oz, and I had watched the scene being filmed, but Darryl and Crank hadn't seen it. If we were lucky, they wouldn't notice.

"Come on," I said, putting the camera back in my pocket. "Hurry!"

I scooted over to the boards and pushed one aside.

"I can't hide in there," hissed Arnie. "I'm scared of small spaces."

I shoved him in. Scrambling after him, I pulled the board back into place.

A beam of light shot through the darkness. In the crack between the boards, I saw Darryl enter the cave, followed by Crank.

Darryl shone a flashlight around. "I don't see them. I'll check the back. You stay here."

He hurried across the boards. Dust drifted down, and I could feel Arnie tense to sneeze. I clapped a hand over his mouth. His shoulders heaved a couple of times, then stopped. He nodded, and I took away my hand.

The boards creaked. I looked up and saw Crank standing on them, directly above us. He checked to the left and the right, squinting to see in the darkness. Then he glanced down, and his eyes opened wide.

He was staring right at me.

I stared back. My neck hurt, and my shoulder was jammed up against Arnie, but I hardly noticed. All I could do was gaze at Crank and shout in my head, "Please don't say anything. Please!"

He kept staring. His lips moved, but nothing came out.

Darryl approached again. "They're not back there," he said. "You see anything?"

Crank gave me one last glance, then looked up at Darryl. "Nothing here."

"Let's get going," said Darryl.

They pounded across the boards and back to the entrance. A moment later they were gone.

Arnie grinned and whispered, "It worked! I used my special X-ray stare to keep him quiet. No one can resist it."

I waited a few minutes just to be safe, then pushed the boards aside. As we climbed out, I checked my watch in the dim light and settled back against the wall.

"Another half hour," I said.

"We can't stay here!" said Arnie. "It's not safe."

"Sure it is. Now that they've checked, it's the last place they'd look."

He squatted down next to me. As he did, there were more footsteps. Arnie looked over at me, but I was already moving. I pulled back the boards.

It was too late. The flashlight beam lit up the cave.

Laura stepped inside.

I don't know why—maybe because I was so relieved—but suddenly I wanted to give her a hug. I threw my arms around her. She pulled me close, then leaned back to look at me.

"What are you doing here?" she asked, her eyes moving from me to Arnie and back again.

"It doesn't matter," I said. "What about you?"

"Darryl asked me to meet him here. He didn't say why."

Arnie said, "You just missed him. He was with Crank."

I wondered why Darryl had invited Laura to the caves. Maybe his investigation had turned up something about Laura. If it had, the caves would be a perfect place to ask her about it, a place where they wouldn't be disturbed.

"What were they doing?" asked Laura.

"Looking for Arnie and me," I said. "It's a long story."

She pulled me close again. When she drew back, her eyes were cold.

"I know," she said. "I know all about it."

"You do?"

Her face contorted, and she screamed, "They're in here!"

My blood ran cold. Just yesterday I had sat across from Laura, feeling as if I had known her forever. Now, like Miles, I was facing a stranger.

I tried to pull away, but her grip was like iron.

"Give me the camera," she said. "I know you've got it."

I said, "I don't understand. What are you doing? Who are you?"

"Agent Laura Burke," she said. "FBI."

Suddenly it all made sense. No wonder she and Darryl had been spending so much time together. They weren't dating—they were on agency business. With her agent's salary she had bought a home. She had been given a standard-issue Plymouth, just like Darryl's except for the color. Meanwhile, lost in my fantasies, I had fallen in love. Arnie wasn't the idiot. I was.

"Laura?" called Darryl from outside the cave. As she turned, Arnie stepped forward and kicked her in the shin. Her grip loosened just long enough for me to twist away.

"Run!" I yelled. We raced back into the darkness, through the space that wasn't a cave but a tunnel, and burst into the open.

The sun had set, but the sky was still glowing. There were stars and a full moon. Somewhere up there was Mars, a world of invaders with flying saucers and death rays. They used to frighten me, but they seemed silly compared with the real thing.

We tore down the gravel road to the parking lot, with Darryl and Laura, taken by surprise, about fifty yards back. I wondered where Crank was. A moment later I got my answer.

"Darryl, they're over here!" he shouted from a hill on the opposite side of the lot. A few moments later Crank appeared beside us, panting.

"That should hold them for a few minutes," he said. "Let's get out of here."

"Whose side are you on?" asked Arnie.

"Shut up," said Crank. I figured that was a good sign. Crank was back, at least for now.

We scrambled up the side of the canyon, hoping that the low-hanging trees and the growing darkness would hide us. When we reached the top, we heard voices below and the rustling of underbrush. I remembered from my map that Beachwood Canyon was just over the rise.

"This way!" I said. We dove down the other side of the hill. Somewhere behind me Crank must have tripped on a limb, because suddenly he went down. We helped him up, but by that time Darryl and Laura were closer, and Crank was limping. At the bottom of the hill, we reached the road.

"I don't know how long I can keep this up," said Crank, his breath ragged.

Then I saw it. Rising up the canyon wall on the far side of the road, shining in the moonlight, was what I'd been looking for—a ribbon of concrete stairs, jutting up the hillside and out of sight.

Miles and Becky had used it. If my plan worked, so would we.

I climbed the stairs, pulling myself up the iron railing with one hand and dragging Crank up with the other. Arnie scampered along behind, pushing Crank and yelling encouragement. When we were halfway up, Darryl and Laura appeared at the bottom. They followed us up the stairs, drawing closer with each step.

I glanced at my watch. "Just a little farther."

"I can't," said Crank.

Arnie gave him a shove, then reared back and slugged him on the arm. "Yes, you can!"

"Hey!" said Crank. He stared at Arnie. Arnie stared right back.

"Now move!" said Arnie.

Crank moved.

Higher and higher we climbed. Darryl and Laura were close enough now that we could see their faces, flat and expressionless.

I checked my watch again. "We're almost there!"

Stumbling, panting, we reached the top. A moment later, so did Darryl and Laura. But they were too late.

Waiting at the top of the stairs, just as I had planned, were Oz and Bernice in the liberalmobile. We piled in and roared off down the street, past Darryl and Laura. Oz rolled down the window.

"Power to the people!" he yelled. And we left them in the dust.

18 · OPEN UP! FBI!

WHEN WE FOUND HIM, HE WAS DRUMMING.

The sound was deeper than before, sad and somehow wiser. We stood outside the door to his house, listening. I had raised my hand to knock but couldn't bring myself to interrupt the low mellow sound.

After we had left Darryl and Laura, there had been no doubt where we would go next. We were full of questions, and only one person could answer them. We told Bernice, and she turned the car toward Altadena.

In the meantime, though, Oz had a question for Crank.

"Why should we trust you?" he demanded.

"I'm sorry," said Crank. "I made a mistake."

"That's it? You made a mistake?"

"He saved us," said Arnie, describing what had happened in the cave.

Crank said, "All I know is, when I was standing there, looking down at you, I couldn't turn you in."

He explained that after he and Darryl had left the cave, Darryl had told him that Laura was an FBI agent.

"She wasn't an actress at all," said Crank. "She was lying to us all along. Both of them were. I didn't want to help them anymore."

"So," said Oz, "you think Feynman's innocent?"

Crank said, "I'm not sure. But I'd like to find out from him, not Darryl."

The drumming stopped. A voice called out from inside the house.

"Is somebody there?"

"It's us," I said. "We'd like to talk with you."

A moment later, Richard Feynman opened the door. He looked older than I remembered. He seemed tired.

Bernice introduced herself. "We're sorry to bother you," she said, "but the boys wanted to see you. They said it's important."

Feynman shrugged. "Come on in."

He stepped aside, and we filed past him into the living room.

"I'm by myself," he said. "My wife went shopping."

In the center of the room was a stool. Next to that was a drum, larger than the bongos he had played in his office. Feynman saw me looking at it.

"That's a conga drum," he said. "They use it in Africa and Cuba. It has a good sound, don't you think?"

"Yes, sir."

He perched on the stool and gestured for us to sit on the sofa. We cleared off some pillows and settled in.

"Professor Feynman," I said, "we have a question for you."

Feynman smiled. "Good. I love questions."

I said, "Why do you have a picture of Klaus Fuchs in your office?"

Feynman stiffened. He gaze darted around the room, then back to me. "He was a friend of mine."

"Was he a good friend?" asked Oz.

"Yes, he was," said Feynman.

"You borrowed his car on weekends," I said. "Isn't that right?"

Feynman stood up. "I can't talk now. I've got things I need to do."

Crank said, "I thought you liked questions."

Bernice, confused, struggled to her feet. "We're sorry, professor. We didn't mean to bother you." She motioned for us to stand, but we didn't move.

"Sir," I said, "we've noticed that you don't like to talk about Los Alamos."

He stared at me, surprised. He wore an expression that I'd seen at home, when I asked questions my father didn't like. The expression said, *Be quiet. We don't talk about that here.*

"You heard the professor," said Bernice. "We need to go."

Arnie jumped to his feet. I pulled him back down.

"Not yet," I said. I looked at my friends. "Right?"

Oz nodded. Arnie whimpered. Crank stuck out his jaw, as if daring someone to hit it.

I turned back to Feynman. "You helped develop the atomic bomb. You were there."

Feynman looked at the floor. He was very still.

Crank said, "Klaus Fuchs was there, too. We know what he was doing. He was a spy."

Feynman didn't move. Then he picked up the conga drum, placed it between his knees, and began to play.

Someone pounded on the door.

"Open up! FBI!"

Instinctively I felt in my pocket. The camera was still there.

Feynman glanced up, alarmed. "Did you bring them here?"

"We didn't mean to," I said. "They must have followed us."

As we watched Feynman, he seemed to make a decision. Getting up from the stool, he went to the door and opened it. Darryl and Laura were standing outside.

"Come in," said Feynman. "I've been wanting to talk to you for a long time."

Darryl shouldered past him, with Laura right behind. She didn't say anything. She didn't even look at me.

Darryl glared at us. "I saw that car out front. I knew you'd be here."

Bernice asked Oz, "Well, aren't you going to introduce us?"

Darryl said, "You're Bernice Feldman. United Nations volunteer. Left-wing activist. Better known around our office as the Donor."

Bernice beamed. "Did you hear that, boys? The FBI knows me."

Laura turned to Feynman. "Professor, I'm afraid my associate has put us in a very awkward position. We've been doing routine checks of the scientists who were at Los Alamos. Your name came up on the list, and he made the mistake of telling these boys."

"I had to," said Darryl. "They were going to blow my cover."

Watching them, I realized that Laura, not Darryl, was the one in charge. She had been running the operation from the beginning. Apparently she was an actress after all.

Laura said, "We weren't planning to approach you like this. Frankly, we didn't want to approach you at all. Then the boys decided to do some investigating of their own."

"They saw the photo of Klaus Fuchs and learned a few other things," said Darryl. "You borrowed his car on weekends. You broke into the master safe at Los Alamos. They thought it seemed suspicious."

Feynman looked at us. I saw anger and disappointment in his face.

"I learned some things myself," said Darryl. "You wrote in

code to your friends. You sneaked out past the guards. Then there was the letter."

"I write lots of letters," snapped Feynman. "Which one are you referring to?"

Darryl shot him a smug grin. "It's from the Soviet embassy, inviting you to Russia for a conference on nuclear physics. How do you explain that, professor?"

The room was silent. Feynman cocked his head. "How did you know about this?"

Darryl glanced at Laura. She said, "We can't answer that. It's classified information."

I reached into my pocket and pulled out the camera. "Here's the answer," I said.

When Darryl saw the camera, his eyes opened wide. He lunged toward me, but Crank blocked his way. Laura shook her head, and Darryl stepped back.

"What's that?" asked Feynman.

"A spy camera," I said. "They took pictures of the letter."

Crank said, "It's my fault. I let him into your office. The letter was on your desk."

Arnie added quickly, "It's okay, though. We stole the camera and got away. Crank helped us."

I handed the camera to Feynman. "You take it. Do what you want with it. We're sorry, professor. We messed up. I hope you're not too mad."

Darryl said, "Give me that. It belongs to the FBI."

"Shut up," said Crank.

Darryl stared at him. Laura watched them grimly. She told Feynman, "Keep the camera. I don't care. Just answer the question."

"What question is that?" he asked.

"How do you explain the letter?"

Feynman gazed at her for the longest time. No one said a word. As I watched him, a terrible thought popped into my head, and I couldn't get rid of it. After all the talk and the chase and the trouble we'd gone to, maybe he really was a spy.

Feynman chuckled. The chuckle turned into a bitter laugh. Without warning, he flipped the camera to Darryl.

"Take it," he said. "I don't want it."

Surprised, Darryl fumbled the camera, then gripped it tightly in his hands.

Feynman turned to Laura. "You people are amazing, you know that? I got the letter on January 13. You know what I did on January 14, the very next day? Huh? Did I show it to my spymaster? Did I check with the Communist Party? No. I wrote the U.S. government, asking if I should go to the conference. I have the letters in my office. Why didn't you find those?"

Laura eyed him skeptically. "Who did you write to?"

"The Atomic Energy Commission. The State Department. Whoever I thought might listen. Months passed. Nobody answered. I was begging the government to look at that letter. Meanwhile, you people broke into my office to see it. Nice work, guys. You're doing a great job."

"That's terrible," said Bernice. "Did you ever hear back?"

"Yeah, finally, a few weeks ago. The head of the Atomic Energy Commission advised me not to go. So I turned down the invitation."

"You said no?" asked Darryl.

"Sure did. In fact, it was in the papers. Do you get the *Los Angeles Times*? The *Washington Post*? Oh, sorry, I forgot. You don't read."

Laura glared at Darryl. "Get me those papers."

"How am I supposed to do that?" he asked.

Feynman said, "Hey, I've got an idea. You know how we can win the Cold War? You two can work for the Russians."

Laura's face turned red. "Look, professor, we botched this. We didn't do our homework. We used poor judgment. We invaded your privacy. I'm afraid we owe you an apology."

"Well?" said Feynman.

"Well what?"

"Let's hear it."

She rolled her eyes. "I'm sorry."

Feynman turned to Darryl.

"Now wait a second," said Darryl. "I admit we were wrong about the letter. But what about the other stuff? The locks, the code, the photo? My God, you were friends with Klaus Fuchs. He spied for the Russians."

I didn't like Darryl, but I had to admit he was asking some good questions. I held my breath, waiting to hear what Feynman would say.

Feynman gave a little wave of his hand. "I like games. I like a mental challenge. Some people work crossword puzzles? I pick locks. I break codes. Sure, I sneaked under the fence at Los Alamos. You know where I went? Can you guess?"

Darryl shook his head.

Feynman said, "Back to the front gate. I wanted to show them how ridiculous their security system was. So I went through the front gate, sneaked out again, went through the front gate, sneaked out. I had a bet with some of my friends about how many times I could walk through the gate before the guards noticed. Five times! I'm telling you, those guards were sharp. Probably friends of yours. They must have thought there were five of me. The Feynman quintuplets."

Darryl wasn't ready to back down. "What about the car?" he asked. "That wasn't a game. It belonged to Klaus Fuchs."

Feynman looked away. "Forget the car. It was nothing."

He always had good answers, up to a point. Then he would get that look on his face and stop. The look told me that something wasn't right. He was holding back. Richard Feynman had a secret.

"Sir," I said, "my friends and I have caused you a lot of trouble. We had this idea that we should investigate you. It was stupid. It was wrong. But while we were investigating, we got to know you. We like you. So can't you just tell us? Why did you borrow the car? Why don't you want to talk about Los Alamos?"

Feynman blinked a few times. He lifted his gaze slowly,

inch by inch, as if it were a thousand-pound weight. Finally his eyes met mine. They were filled with pain.

"I won't tell him," said Feynman, nodding toward Darryl, "but I'll tell you."

I waited. We all waited.

"It was because of Arline," he said.

19 · THE BOMB

"HER NAME WAS ARLINE GREENBAUM," SAID FEYNMAN. "I met her in high school. She had blue eyes and beautiful wavy hair. She liked to smile. I liked to watch her. It was mostly from a distance, though. After all, what did I know about girls?

"She played the piano. She used to teach my sister Joan. Finally I worked up the nerve to talk to her. Before you knew it, we were going to movies and even a dance or two. When I went off to college at MIT, she would take the train to see me on weekends.

"She loved me. Can you believe it? By the time I started graduate school at Princeton, we were planning to get married. Then she got sick. It took the doctors a while, but finally they figured it out. She had TB—a rare kind called lymphatic tuberculosis. There was no known cure."

Feynman shook his head. He walked to a window and peered outside, as if looking for Arline. Then, turning, he smiled at me.

"You know what? We got married anyway. The doctors said she was contagious, but I didn't care. We'd be careful. We'd go through it together.

"That was 1942. The war had started. The government had this crazy idea that the way to win was to put a bunch of scientists on a mountaintop in New Mexico. To run the place, they got a fellow named J. Robert Oppenheimer—Oppie, we called him. They told us to invent a new kind of bomb, using atomic power.

"When Oppie hired me, I asked him, why New Mexico? You know what he said? He had suffered from TB as a kid and had gone there for a cure. New Mexico was famous for it. Can you imagine that? So Arline and I packed up our things and went out west. I moved to Los Alamos. Arline went to a hospital in Albuquerque, a hundred miles away."

Feynman walked over to a coffee table. He picked up a deck of cards and shuffled it a couple of times.

"I used to know some card tricks," he said. "I learned a few as a kid, and I'd do them for the people at Los Alamos."

He fanned out the cards and held them in front of Oz. "Pick one. Look at the card, but don't tell me. Then put it back."

Oz did as he was told. Feynman squared up the deck, then looked through it. He selected a card and showed it to Oz. "Is this it?"

Oz smiled awkwardly. "Actually, no."

"Well," said Feynman, "what do you know."

He put the cards back on the table.

"It used to work," he said.

"That's okay," said Arnie. "I'm sure it was great."

Feynman said, "It's just a game. It's something you do when you're bored and stuck out in the middle of nowhere."

"Sort of like codes?" I said.

He nodded. "I wrote to Arline every day. I knew the censors were reading our mail, so we invented a code. It gave her something to do."

"Did they let you visit her?" I asked.

"On weekends," said Feynman. "Only problem was, I didn't have a car."

Oz said, "So you borrowed one from Klaus Fuchs."

Feynman nodded. "He always asked about Arline. He really cared. Klaus was my friend."

"You didn't know he was a spy?" asked Crank.

"Klaus? He was a sweet, simple guy. When I found out about him after the war, I couldn't believe it." He smiled sadly. "When I visited Arline, I felt as if I was leading a double life. I never knew Klaus was too."

Arnie said, "I don't understand. You're married. Your wife is still alive."

"She's my second wife," said Feynman. "Arline died of TB."

Laura gazed at Feynman, a pained expression on her face. "I think we've got everything we need. I'm sorry, professor. I'm sorry about everything."

She motioned to Darryl, and he followed her out the door.

Bernice got up from the sofa. "Come on, boys. We should go."

"Do they have to?" asked Feynman. I looked at him, surprised. He seemed small and lonely.

I said to Bernice, "Maybe we should stay."

"You could leave the boys here," Feynman told her. "I'll drive them home when my wife gets back."

Bernice looked at us, not sure what to do.

Oz said, "It's fine, Mom."

She leaned over and kissed him on the cheek, then turned to Feynman. "I'm sorry about Arline. She must have been a wonderful girl."

After Bernice left, Oz said, "I wish I could have met her."

"We had fun," said Feynman. "That was the strange thing. She was dying, and we had a great time. For our wedding anniversary she gave me a grill, an apron, and a chef's hat. We set it up outside the hospital, right next to a busy street, and I grilled some steaks. People would laugh and point. Some of them honked. I got embarrassed. She told me the same thing she always said: 'What do you care what other people think?'"

He shook his head. "Isn't that something? I was trying to help her, but she was the one who turned out to be strong."

Feynman picked up the deck of cards. He thumbed through it, then set it back on the table.

"She died in June 1945," he said. "In July we tested the first atomic bomb. In August we used it on Hiroshima. I know I didn't really kill Arline. But when I picture all those people dying, I think of her too."

He sat down on the stool, pulled the conga drum to him, and played. The beat was slow. It pulsed in the darkness.

After a while he stopped and looked up at me. "Want to try it?"

"Sure," I said.

I took his place on the stool. He showed me how to hold the drum between my knees. I tapped it with my fingertips while my friends watched.

"Put your fingers together," said Feynman. "Use your thumbs, like this."

I tried it. The sound was stronger.

He said, "Now hit it, hard."

I did.

"As hard as you can," he said. "You won't hurt it."

I hit it again and again. On the drumhead I pictured Darryl, then Laura, then my stupid little sister, then my dad. I pictured the pod people in the movie and in my life, who turned away from hard decisions, who avoided pain at all costs, who would rather be comfortable than human. I saw them on the drumhead, staring back at me. Maybe I was one of them.

I hit the drum again, hard. When I looked up, Arnie was watching me. "Your face is all red."

"It feels good, doesn't it?" said Feynman.

The others tried it. They were no better than I was, but somehow in their playing you could tell how they were feeling—Oz thoughtful, Crank determined, Arnie nervous.

Then Feynman took the drum again. As he spoke, he played.

"At first I was excited that we had dropped the bomb. We all were. We'd been working on it night and day for three years. Then I started thinking about all those people in Hiroshima. I killed thousands. Some were vaporized in an instant. Some were crushed or blown apart. Some survived the blast and died slowly from the inside, like Arline. What was the difference, really? She was dead. They were dead. Maybe I had killed them all."

"It wasn't your fault," said Arnie.

"Wasn't it? You know, when my friends and I agreed to build the bomb, we thought Hitler was working on one. We were acting in self-defense, right? We had no choice. Then Germany surrendered. Did we stop working on the bomb? Did we pause even once to ask why we were doing it? No. We just put our heads down and kept working. When we looked up, all those people were dead."

The beat slowed down and stopped. Feynman set the drum aside.

"I left Los Alamos in October. Right after that, I had lunch with my mother in New York City. We were at a restaurant on Fifty-ninth Street. I knew that if the bomb were dropped downtown, it would kill us and everything for miles around. Afterward we went for a walk, and I saw a crew of workers building a bridge. I thought, 'Why do they bother? Don't they know? It's all going to be destroyed.'"

"You think it will?" I asked.

"Sometimes I do," said Feynman. "What do you think?"

I looked at Arnie. "It scares me."

"It scares a lot of people," said Feynman. "Maybe that's good."

Crank said, "You won the war. It was the bomb that did it."

Feynman shook his head. "It wasn't the bomb. It was fear that won the war. That's what we made at Los Alamos. We set it loose on the world. It's still out there. You read it in newspapers. You hear it in Congress. You see it in horror movies. Fear. Dread. Terror."

"Is it really that bad?" I asked.

Feynman gazed at me, a haunted expression on his face. "Yes, it is," he said. "We'll never get away from it now."

20 · A BRIGHT RED ROSE

WHEN FEYNMAN DROPPED ME OFF AT HOME, IT WAS GETTING LATE. The house was dark except for one lamp in the living room. I went inside and I found my mother sitting next to it. Her cheeks were wet. In her hand was a twisted handkerchief.

"I didn't mean to worry you," I said.

She looked up at me, puzzled, then noticed the handkerchief. "This? Oh, it wasn't you, Paul. Bernice called when I was putting Lulu to bed. She told me you were fine."

"Then what's wrong?" I asked.

She patted the sofa next to her, the way she used to do when I was little. I sat down beside her. She blew her nose, and we sat there in silence.

"Your father and I are having some problems," she said finally.

"Problems?"

"You may have noticed, he's not a happy man. He wasn't happy to start with, and then he got that job." She shook her head. "Everything's secret. He can't talk about it. I ask him how his day went, and he just stares at me. He was always quiet, but this is different. We live in a deep freeze."

She put her arm around me. We sat there quietly. After a while she said, "Did you know that your father used to tell jokes?"

"Dad?"

"The first time we met, he squeezed my hand as if he was milking it. He said, 'Hi, I'm a dairy farmer.'"

I tried to imagine it. All I could see was that worried look on his face.

She said, "I've asked him to quit his job, but he won't. He says it would be too hard. We wouldn't have as much money. We might have to sell the house. But so what? We'd get by somehow."

"What are we going to do?" I said.

"I've already done it. I asked him to leave."

"Leave?"

"He's gone, Paul. Tonight he packed his things and moved out. Your father and I are getting a divorce."

Divorce. It was a harsh, hollow-sounding word. What did it really mean?

"I thought you loved each other," I said.

Her eyes welled up. She wiped them with her handkerchief.

"That's the sad part," she said. "We do. But he loves his TV more."

Thinking about my father and his job reminded me

of Feynman. *I killed thousands*, he had said. Maybe he had. Maybe we all had. Arline, the people in Hiroshima—we were killing them every day. We tried to do better, but we didn't. Parents got divorced. People died. That's just the way it was.

Meanwhile, we went to the movies. We watched thirty-foot spiders and radioactive zombies. We screamed and cowered. But the scariest part wasn't the monsters. It wasn't the Russians or the bomb. It wasn't out there. It was in here. It was inside of us. Inside of me.

"I'm glad you've got your friends," said my mother. "You can still have fun."

I thought of Oz, Arnie, Crank, and me, running from the pod people, investigating Feynman, hearing about Arline. Fun? Is that what we were having?

My mother leaned over. Kissing me on the forehead, she said, "We'll be fine. You'll see."

"I hope so," I said.

She put away her handkerchief and got up from the sofa. "You know, it's dark in here."

Walking over, she flipped a switch, and the lights came up. The house was still black and white. But in the center of the room, resting on the coffee table, was something new. It was a small vase. In the vase was a bright red rose.

It wasn't a normal movie premiere. For one thing, it didn't happen in Hollywood. The premiere was five miles south, at the Warner Theater in downtown Los Angeles. There was no row of limousines or parade of stars. There was just one spotlight, operated by a tired old man who kept stopping to talk to kids.

Still, it seemed like a pretty big deal to us. The front of the theater was crowded with people. The manager had roped off the entrance to create a walkway to the street, and he waited proudly at the curb.

It was a warm September night. Six months had passed since we had learned the truth about Richard Feynman. In the weeks following, we had stopped by his house a few times to talk and play the drums. He seemed to enjoy the company. Over the summer my mother had filed for divorce. Lulu and I saw our father on weekends, and he was as tense as ever. That fall, Arnie, Crank, Oz, and I had started eighth grade, which meant Mrs. Kramer wasn't our social studies teacher anymore. Personally, I missed her. No one could do a drop drill like Mrs. Kramer.

A couple of weeks after school had started, Oz had read about the premiere in the *Hollywood Reporter*, and our parents had given us permission to go. Crank was with us, though we hadn't been seeing much of him recently. Things didn't feel the same between us. Maybe they never would. For once, I wasn't trying to smooth it over.

Bernice, whose sister lived nearby, had scheduled a visit and dropped us off on the way. As she drove off in the liberalmobile, Arnie, Crank, and I looked up at the theater marquee, while Oz checked out the crowd.

"Wow," said Arnie, "*Invasion of the Body Snatchers*. It's a real movie."

Crank grunted. "Movies aren't real."

"This one is," said Arnie.

Oz, meanwhile, had found a place for us to stand. He led us through the crowd to an open area right next to where the cars would pull up.

"Hey, this is great," I said.

"I'm hungry," said Arnie. "You think they have PEZ?"

To Arnie, the world was a giant PEZ dispenser. He hurried off to check, while the rest of us joined the crowd looking for celebrities. A few minutes later a Ford convertible pulled up, and Don Siegel got out with an attractive, well-dressed woman.

"Sorry," the manager told him. "This is for movie people."

Oz tapped the manager on the shoulder. "Sir," he said, "maybe you didn't recognize him. This is Don Siegel, the director of the film."

The manager's eyebrows shot up. "Mr. Siegel, of course. Welcome to the Warner Theater."

Looking past the manager, Siegel grinned at Oz. "Glad you could make it. Where are you sitting?"

"Uh, we're not sure yet," said Oz.

Siegel turned to the manager. "These boys are with us. They'll need reserved seats."

"Yes, sir! Our pleasure, sir."

Siegel winked at us and moved off toward the entrance.

A moment later, Walter Wanger arrived in a Lincoln Continental. The crowd buzzed. They didn't know him, but they recognized an expensive suit when they saw one. Sherwin Gray, the studio executive, was with him. They were followed shortly by Ted Haworth, inventor of the pods, and Frederick Ellsworth, the cameraman.

"Where are the stars?" a little boy whined to his mother. "You said there would be stars."

A little girl called out, "Daddy, look at that long car!"

Following her gaze, we saw it—the one limousine of the evening. It was a few years old, with dents on the side and a missing hood ornament. A chauffeur in a scruffy uniform got out and opened the doors. Kevin McCarthy and Dana Wynter emerged, smiling brightly, followed by their co-stars King Donovan and Carolyn Jones.

Oz said, "Low-budget film, low-budget limo."

The crowd surged forward. Kids called out for autographs, including the little boy and his mother. The four stars signed for a few minutes, then headed inside.

As they left, I saw Arnie approach, holding a PEZ dispenser high for us to see. "They had the space trooper! I've been looking everywhere for this."

As he fiddled with the space trooper, cars continued to arrive, bringing the cast and crew. Among the cars was Laura's blue Plymouth. When she climbed out, our eyes met briefly. She looked away and kept walking.

I turned to my friends. "I'll meet you guys inside."

I caught up with her next to the entrance. Not sure of what to say, I noticed a stack of programs nearby and picked one up.

"Can I have your autograph?" I asked.

She stopped and turned around. Her face glowed, as beautiful as ever. "Hello, Paul."

I held out the program. "I really would like an autograph."

"Why?" she said. "You already have one."

I shrugged. "For old time's sake."

She looked at me, puzzled, then took a pen from her purse and signed the program. As I watched her, I thought back to that first autograph. A lot had happened since then.

She handed the program back, and I looked at her signature. It was small and neat, the writing of a person who likes to be in control.

"I'm sorry about the way things worked out," she said.

"You were doing your job."

"I lied. It's a part of the job I don't like."

"Where's Darryl?" I asked.

Her eyes sparkled. "He was reassigned. As we speak, he's hard at work in Butte, Montana."

The way she said it, I had a feeling she hadn't been sorry to see him go.

"I saw the two of you arguing," I said. "I guess you didn't always agree on things."

She snorted. "Darryl went into the wrong profession. He should have been a cowboy."

"What about you?" I asked. "You really could be an actress."

"That's very sweet," she said, "but I've got more important things to do."

I said, "You really believe that stuff, don't you? Us against them. Good versus evil. The good guys and the bad guys."

"It's all true," she said. "History will prove it. You'll see."

We probably would never meet again. Maybe that's what gave me the courage to say it.

"I thought I loved you," I said.

Her expression softened. "Really?"

"I didn't know you at all, did I?"

"You knew part of me."

I shook my head. "It's not enough."

"You deserve more," she said. "You'll get it someday."

Another cast member called out to her. She looked around. "I have to go. I'm about to appear in my first and last movie."

She gazed at me for a moment. Then she leaned over, kissed me on the cheek, and was gone.

I found Oz, Crank, and Arnie in the tenth row center, behind Don Siegel. Oz handed me a box of popcorn, and the movie started.

It was all there—Miles, Becky, the pod people. They lived in my town, Sierra Madre. They pounded through the streets, up the staircase, and into the cave. There, Miles looked into Becky's face and saw a stranger. He recoiled in horror. So did I.

Fear was alive. You could see it in people's eyes. You could hear it in their voices. It was out there, black, blank, floating at the edge of the world. It was gathering force, getting ready to strike.

There was one way to stop it. Ask questions. Face the answers. Learn the truth, even if it hurts. When you get stuck, grab a drum and play.

At the end of the movie, Miles escaped to a hospital and told a doctor about the pod people. The doctor assumed he was crazy. But while they spoke, an accident victim was brought in. He had been hit by a truck full of strange objects that looked like giant seedpods.

The doctor stared in amazement. He yelled to an attendant, "Get on your radio and sound an all-points alarm. It's an emergency!"

In front of me, Don Siegel shook his head. He had been forced to tack on a happy ending. The studio had gotten its way.

The movie wasn't as good as it could have been. Maybe nothing ever is. But you know what? It still scared the pee out of us.

When the last scene ended, the lights came up.

"I love it," said Oz.

"I feel sick," said Arnie.

"Shut up," said Crank.

I just smiled.

AUTHOR'S NOTE

WHEN I WAS A BOY, WE FOUGHT THE WAR ON TERROR EVERY SATURDAY AT THE MOVIES. The lights went down, and monsters jumped off the screen and into our world. There were dinosaurs, zombies, giant spiders, and radioactive bugs.

To me, the most terrifying of all were the pod people in the 1956 classic, *Invasion of the Body Snatchers*. This low-budget film, shot in black and white, was based on a story by Jack Finney and directed by Don Siegel. The American Film Institute has named it one of the one hundred most thrilling films ever made.

Why were there so many horror movies in the 1950s? Because we were scared—of the Russians, of flying saucers, and especially of the bomb. The first atomic bomb was dropped in 1945. The first hydrogen bomb, a hundred times more destructive, was set off in 1952. Every day in the papers we saw news of our impending destruction; it seemed only natural to look for it in movies, too.

Invasion of the Body Snatchers was shot in the spring of 1955 in the sleepy little town of Sierra Madre, California. Just a few miles away, in Altadena, lived Richard Feynman, one of the century's true geniuses and an inventor of the atomic bomb. These two facts, seemingly unrelated, fired my imagination, and I began to wonder what it would have been like to live there. Out of that thought came Oz, Arnie, Crank, and Paul—joking, spying, shaking in their shoes.

Those four characters and their families are fictional, as are Laura Burke, Darryl Gibbons, Sherwin Gray, and the indomitable Mrs. Kramer. Virtually all the others, along with most of the events around which I wove this story, were real and are used fictitiously here to provide a backdrop for the novel.

Director Don Siegel created a science fiction masterpiece in *Invasion of the Body Snatchers* and then was in fact pressured by nervous studio executives to change it by adding a prologue and epilogue. In the film, extras chased Kevin McCarthy and Dana Wynter through the streets of Sierra Madre, up the stairs of Beachwood Canyon, and into the caves of Griffith Park.

Richard Feynman, while working on the bomb at Los Alamos, visited his wife Arline on weekends. She died in 1945, two months before Hiroshima. For years afterward, Feynman and his colleagues on the Manhattan Project were followed by FBI agents. You can read the FBI reports on Feynman, as I did, by requesting his file under the Freedom of Information Act. In January of 1955, while Ted Haworth was scouting movie locations in Sierra Madre, Feynman received an invitation from the Soviet embassy to attend a physics meeting in Moscow. A loyal American, he contacted the government and waited months for a reply. Finally, on their advice, he declined the invitation. Feynman had mixed emotions about his work at Los Alamos. The doubts he expresses in my story are based on stories he himself told.

As amazing as it may sound to modern-day tourists, Hollywood Boulevard in 1955 was a place where kids could safely spend the afternoon. I know, because my friends and I did exactly that in the early 1960s. We went to movies, compared handprints with the stars at Grauman's Chinese Theater, browsed in Pickwick Bookshop, and ate hot fudge sundaes at C. C. Brown's. We tried sneaking into Frederick's of Hollywood but were hustled out the door.

The characters I encountered in my research led remarkable lives, extending far beyond the events of 1955.

Richard Feynman remained at Cal Tech for the rest of his career. He did pioneering work on a wide range of topics, including quantum mechanics, superfluidity, nanotechnology, and quarks. He shared the Nobel Prize for physics in 1965. After the space shuttle exploded in 1986, he was named to the Challenger Commission and made the news by dropping an O-ring into a glass of ice water to demonstrate the cause of the explosion. Feynman, divorced from his second wife in 1956, found happiness once again with his third wife,

Gweneth, and their children, Carl and Michelle.

Jirayr Zorthian was a close friend of Feynman's and a long-standing and eccentric member of Altadena's artistic community. He used recycled materials to build a hillside home and ranch. For years he held a summer camp there so that local children could experience nature, the excitement of creativity, and the joy of learning.

Don Siegel went on to have a long and distinguished directing career, including the classic films *The Shootist*, *Escape from Alcatraz*, and *Dirty Harry*, one of several he made with actor Clint Eastwood. Eastwood, a great director in his own right, dedicated his Academy Award–winning film *Unforgiven* to Siegel, whom he considered a mentor.

Walter Wanger, who produced *Invasion of the Body Snatchers* and several other low-budget films after his release from prison, gradually worked his way back up the Hollywood ladder, eventually achieving success with *I Want to Live!* Unfortunately, he followed that up a few years later with the big-budget disaster *Cleopatra*, from which he never recovered.

Ted Haworth, after making giant seedpods and plaster casts for *Invasion of the Body Snatchers*, lent his creativity to a wide variety of films, including *The Naked and the Dead*, *Some Like It Hot*, and *The Longest Day*. He won five Academy Awards for art direction.

Sam Peckinpah parlayed his role as actor and dialog director in *Invasion of the Body Snatchers* into a long and successful directing career. He started off doing Westerns on television with *Gunsmoke* and *The Rifleman*, then added blood and guts to the mix in his landmark film *The Wild Bunch*.

Kevin McCarthy, recipient of an Academy Award nomination for his work in the 1951 movie *Death of a Salesman*, continues to act on stage, screen, and television. He had a cameo appearance in the 1978 remake of *Invasion of the Body Snatchers*.

Dana Wynter, born in Germany and brought up in England, appeared in dozens of films and television shows, eventually retiring to Scotland, where she still spends a portion of her time.

King Donovan enjoyed a career as one of the busiest actors in Hollywood. He often played bookish intellectuals, and over the years he carved out a special niche in such creepy classics such as *Beast from 20,000 Fathoms* and the *Night Gallery* television series.

Carolyn Jones was a familiar face in movies during the 1950s and 1960s, but she is probably most famous for her role as Morticia in the hit television series *The Addams Family*.

It wasn't easy to write a story connecting horror movies, physics, and the FBI. When I tried to describe the idea, I got lots of funny looks. Luckily, a few people understood and offered to help.

Debby Henderson of the Sierra Madre Library and Historical Archives dug up newspaper articles and publications of the time. Rob and Laurie Tribken helped me locate Sierra Madre residents who had been present at the filming. One of those residents, Marjorie Peterson of Mama Pete's Nursery School, had taken home movies of the filming and was kind enough to share them with me, along with her memories of that time.

I received invaluable help from the staff of the Margaret Herrick Library of the Academy of Motion Picture Arts and Sciences, as well as of the Altadena, Pasadena, Hollywood, and Los Angeles public libraries.

During my research I read many fine books but none as helpful and inspiring as James Gleick's *Genius: The Life and Science of Richard Feynman*.

I'm deeply indebted to my editors, Alexandra Cooper and Alyssa Eisner Henkin, and my agents, Jodi Reamer and Amy Berkower. Most of all, I'm grateful for the continuing love and support of my wife, Yvonne Martin Kidd, and my daughter, Maggie.